BOXERS OR BRIEFS

HALEY RHOADES

HR

Haley Rhoades

Author

Paperback ISBN-13: 978-0-9989590-4-7

Paperback ISBN-10: 0-9989590-4-9

❀ Created with Vellum

Special Thanks to my husband for letting me live my dream even if it means I am writing all night.
If you were a book you'd be a BEST SELLER.

INFORMATION ON TOPICS

For more information on topics in Boxers or Briefs:

Juvenile Diabetes Research Foundation: http://www.jdrf.org/

Post-Traumatic Stress Disorder: https://www.ptsd.va.gov/public/where-to-get-help.asp

Survivors of a Suicide Loss: http://www.suicidology.org/suicide-survivors/suicide-loss-survivors

TO ENHANCE YOUR READING:

Check out the Trivia Page
at the end of the book
before reading Chapter #1.

No Spoilers—I promise.

ACKNOWLEDGMENTS

Special thanks to Jade Borg and Annie Woods for all your words of wisdom and support. Facebook Writing Groups brought us together. A Big thank you to the Facebook Writing/Author Groups for answering questions, challenging me, and honing my craft.

PROLOGUE

My dorm room walls close in on me. I struggle to breathe the dense air. Red flows everywhere. It stains the curtains, the blinds, the blankets, the bookshelves, the desk, the floor. Everything crimson as everything is bloodstained. My wails pierce the quiet room. I turn my hands over. Blood drips from my fingertips. Her blood. Leslie's blood. Everywhere I look--Leslie's blood. I cannot catch my breath. No matter how hard I try, I can't pull in enough air.

My eyes fly open. A nightmare. *Will they ever stop?*

I left college to escape the constant memories. Everywhere I went I was attacked by memories of Leslie. I left my family and hers in Hannibal to avoid catching her reflection in the local ice cream parlor window only to turn around and again realize she isn't there. I abandoned everything I'd known since the age of twelve. I needed a new start. I loved Leslie. I will always love her. I couldn't take the constant pain of a life without Leslie in a world of memories of her.

I packed my bags, loaded them in my brother's car, and ran away in the middle of the night. In my new town, I can make new memories. In my new city, nothing reminds me of Leslie. Our friends, our boyfriends, even our parents don't know where I am. Only my little brother Jack knows my new cell number.

In my new life, the panic attacks are fewer; the nightmares are less frequent. However, the pain the dreams bring hasn't dissipated. I untangle myself from my twisted sheets. No need to remain in bed, I never sleep after a nightmare.

CHAPTER ONE

Ali:

I jump as my ringing phone pulls me from my book-world back to my real world. As my character friends hide once again in the pages of the novel, I bolt to the bedroom and answer my cell phone. In stereotypical fashion, I left my phone on the charger in my haste to vanish into my book as I do so often these days. After breakfast, I chose to curl up on my ratty sofa in my pajamas with my current book. With nothing planned on this Friday, I quickly lost track of time in my world of cool chicks and hot alpha males.

"Hello," I greet, noting it is now one-fifteen in the afternoon.

"Ali, I have a job for you," Gloria shares. "Can you stop by the agency before five today to discuss it?"

I quickly scan my current state of dress, then inform her I can stop by in an hour or so. Gloria is awesome. She knows my desperate situation and saves the best assignments for me. While she isn't old enough to be my mother, she assumes the role anyway. Alone in this new city, I allow her. I need someone to help me as I start down a new path.

I hop from the sofa, abandoning the e-reader, then dart to the bathroom for a shower and to dress. Although I prefer my book world where every girl gets the guy, I reside in the real world where I need money to pay my bills. As I shower, I mentally tally the unpaid bills on my dresser. I always pay rent first. I paid electric and gas last month, so I need to pay my cell phone and restock the cabinets this month.

In a perfect world, I would hold a job in which I work enough hours to earn the money I need to cover all my monthly bills. I gave up on luxuries and entertainment months ago. When I decided I couldn't attend college another day, couldn't face my parents with their judgments or concerns any longer and didn't want to burden my boyfriend with my screwed-up head, I gave up everything to start anew.

I thank mother nature for providing this beautiful April day, so I may walk the ten blocks to the agency. It's one less trip for my decrepit car, Gertrude, to attempt. Referring to Gertrude as a car is a bit of a stretch, her best years were before 2010. Duct tape holds her back bumper in place, a bungee cord secures the trunk, the passenger door opens only from the inside, and the crack in the windshield threatens to spread soon. She is all I have, all I can afford, and she is better than no car.

Gloria's giant grin greets me the minute I enter. "There's my girl," she squeals while rising to embrace me in a tight hug. "What were you doing on this beautiful Friday?"

I shrug. I don't want to admit I was holed up in my apartment, on my ratty sofa, in my pajamas, reading a romance book. I hope Gloria imagines me taking a walk in the park or reading on a park bench.

She escorts me to the small conference room with her laptop in hand. Upon sitting, she immediately begins describing the opportunity she found for me.

It seems the Lennox Law Firm needs a receptionist to cover an employee maternity leave for six to eight weeks. The hours will be eight a.m. to one p.m. each weekday and the pay is $13 an hour.

Perfect! Five hours a day times 5 days times $13 is $325 a week. A steady income of $300 a week will allow me to pay all my bills every month. Maybe I can even buy some peanut butter and bread instead of just eating ramen twice a day.

"Earth to Ali," Gloria teases calling my attention back toward her. "Monday?"

"Umm," I have no idea what she said.

"Can you start Monday at eight?" she asks again while smiling a knowing smile—the temporary job means a lot to me.

I reply I can indeed begin on Monday. She asks me to sign the form and hands me information on the position to take with me.

"I'm alone tomorrow evening, would you like to come over to dinner?" Gloria asks while tilting her head. Hope written all over her face, she continues. "We could watch a movie and chat."

Of course, I don't need to check my calendar. "Yes, what can I bring?" I respond. A little bud of excitement glimmers in my belly.

"Bring nothing," Gloria states. "I have meat in the freezer and all the fixings for us to make cookies. I'll pick you up about three—we can bake and grill together."

I squeeze Gloria's hands in mine while words evade me. I fight the tears that threaten to form. I'm sure she knows just how much I long for a friend and need to get out of my tiny apartment.

"Gloria line three is for you," hollers the receptionist from the front desk.

As Gloria excuses herself to take the call at her desk, I attempt to gather myself before I start the walk back home. I wave at the receptionist before I pull the front door open.

"Ali, wait!" Gloria's voice causes me to freeze in place.

I release the door, turn toward Gloria, and find she is still on the phone with her free arm frantically waving me toward her. Slowly I move her way.

"Yes. I see. Yes," Gloria responds to the caller. "I have the perfect person for you." She winks at me. "Yes, organized and won't need supervision. Okay, I'll email the forms. Look them over, sign them and send them back by Monday afternoon. I'll have someone there for you on Tuesday. No, thank you. Good-bye."

I hope Gloria realizes she already booked me for next Tuesday. Surely, she didn't forget in the five minutes since I exited the conference room.

"What would you say if I told you I have a second task for you that allows you to keep the legal job and earn more money?" Gloria taunts.

"Yes, please," I quickly beg.

"A gym needs office and bookkeeping help two days a week for two to three hours at $13 an hour," she squeals. Gloria is as excited for me as I am.

"If I can make it work, I want them both," I state.

Gloria explains she arranged for me to work Tuesday and Thursday afternoons starting at two. The client stated I can decide if I need to work until four or five each day. He seems desperate and very flexible. I take a nearby chair while I wait for her to print out a form for me to sign on this position. With my two placement detail sheets in hand, I head to my apartment to plan for next week.

As soon as I enter the apartment, I grab a notepad and figure my potential earnings. Three hours times two days times $13 is $78 added to $325 is $403 a week. Heck Yeah! Now I can buy jelly this month, too.

CHAPTER TWO

Ali:

Monday morning finds me anxious and excited. I rise an hour earlier than needed to be sure I am ready for the first day at the law firm. Many times, over the weekend, I thanked God I brought my entire wardrobe with me. I select a gray pencil skirt, royal blue silk blouse, and gray heels for my first day in such a professional setting.

I took an internship at a local accounting firm the summer between sophomore and junior year of college. My parents bought me 'appropriate attire' for the office. No matter how often I informed my parents I planned to work in a relaxed office post-graduation, they protested the cute, fashionable summer dresses I wanted to wear. I would never hear the end of it if they could see me right now.

Even though the drive will be fifteen minutes with morning traffic, I leave at seven. I park in the parking garage then walk a block in the opposite direction of the law firm to a coffee shop. I assume my spot in the long line of morning caffeine worshipers while browsing social media. Although I no longer post, I occasionally look in on my former friends on Snapchat and Instagram. I place my phone in my purse. I don't miss college. I don't miss the frat parties, the finals, studying in the library, or the he-said/she-said garbage.

Eventually, it's my turn to order. I place my order for an iced-cappuccino and muffin then proceed to the cash register to pay. While waiting for them to call my name, I mentally calculate the decline in my account. I don't often treat myself, I'm starting two new jobs this week, so I splurge. I enjoy my breakfast treat as I walk toward my new job.

I exit the elevator on the fifth floor and immediately find myself in the law office. The reception desk sits empty. I glance at my phone—it is 7:50. I choose to sit on a chair with a direct view of the front desk. I turn off my ringer and place my cell phone in my purse. I tug my pencil skirt toward my knees then play with the buttons on my blouse, ensuring I didn't miss any this morning.

A few moments pass before the woman who must be Ray, the one I'm covering for, appears from the back-office apologizing for keeping me waiting. Pregnant is an understatement. She's enormous and looks ready to pop any minute.

As Ray gives me a tour of the back office, I marvel at the opulence and prestige it boasts. Rich mahogany furniture graces the conference room. The large table can comfortably seat twenty. Shelf after shelf of legal books populate the bookshelves lining an entire wall. Floor-to-ceiling windows display a grand view from this height. Next door, Marshall and Stephen Lennox's closed office doors have the blinds drawn, piquing my curiosity. I'd like to see how lavish they are. I've never met with an attorney, so I am curious.

Tyson Lennox's office door stands open, and his assistant permits us to peek inside. His office is about the size of my apartment. Really. A mahogany desk faces us complete with a matching credenza behind it on the wall. A high back leather chair with shiny gold tacks along the sides awaits its mighty lawyer to return. He too has a marvelous view via the floor to ceiling wall of windows. Two comfortable chairs face his desk while a seating area near the door contains a black leather sofa with two matching side chairs. I wonder how much the furniture in a single lawyer's office costs. I can probably live for a year on that sum.

Ray explains she will demonstrate typical tasks for an hour or so while she answers my questions. Then I will take a stab at it with Ray nearby to jump in if needed.

I take detailed notes in my spiral notebook as Ray answers the phones with her wireless headset. I wear a headset plugged directly into the phone so that I can hear the calls. As staff and lawyers arrive near nine o'clock, Ray introduces me to each.

Around ten, I start answering incoming calls. Ray ensures I press the right extension before I transfer each caller. Although the phone lines seem to ring continuously, I handle the switchboard easily. Ray takes back answering the switchboard while she explains other tasks I will perform daily like mail, data entry, coffee, lunch orders, and other items the staff might request of me. All in all, I leave at one and feel I am up to this challenging position.

Many times, temp jobs are boring. Some positions I answered one phone call every half hour, filed, or sat at a desk in case a customer walked in. I prefer to keep busy. I like a challenge. I will look forward to my time here each morning.

Ali: I am going to love, love, love working at the law firm.
Jack: Nice you finally have a placement you like.
Ali: It is fast paced. The staff seem nice.
Ali: And it pays great too.
Jack: When do you start boxing?
Ali: I AM NOT boxing. I start working at the gym tomorrow at 2.
Ali: I'm nervous about that one.
Jack: Why?
Ali: It's just the unknown. Not sure what I will be doing while there.
Jack: Well if you get bored you can box.
Ali: Ha Ha
Jack: I'm serious
Ali: I know you are. Gotta go my ramen is ready.
Jack: My big sis the gourmet chef

Ali: 🩶

On Tuesday morning, I am much less anxious and nervous. My excitement grows the closer I come to the firm. I quickly secure my purse in the file drawer, place the headset on my ear, and assume my position at the reception desk. As staff and lawyers arrive, I greet each with a smile, a greeting, or a wave if I'm on a call.

Marshall Lennox makes me promise to inform his assistant or himself if I need anything or have any questions. He is a tall, plump man dressed impeccably in a pinstriped suit.

I'm on the phone transferring a call to Stephen Lennox when Tyson Lennox arrives, so I wave. He breezes by me with no response. I shrug it off as a busy man on a mission. I can't fault anyone with work on their mind. Stephen informs me Ray had her baby last night and both are doing fine. He teases that she felt so comfortable with me covering for her that she relaxed, and the baby popped right out. I write on a sticky-note to send flowers and a card from the staff to her hospital.

The morning flies by, and before I know it, the staff starts heading to lunch. The computer monitor informs me it is now 11:45. Caller after caller, I transfer to the team inside the inner office. It amazes me how alone it feels in the reception area with a wall and large glass doors separating the spaces.

"One moment," I state to a caller. I look at my notes, "Stephen is in court, I can transfer you... Okay, thank you." Then I transfer them to Stephen's extension. I startle when I glance up from the switchboard.

"Hello," Tyson snaps. "Do you know who I am?"

I find it odd that he walked to reception to have this unpleasant conversation with a temp on her first day alone. "Hello, Mr. Lennox," I greet with a smile. I attempt to kill him with kindness.

"Ha, nice one," he retorts. "I know you are aware by now that three Mr. Lennox that work here."

I don't speak—I merely nod.

10

"I am Tyson Lennox." He points to his chest, reiterating he is Tyson. "I would appreciate it if you could stop sending Stephen's calls to my extension. This morning, I have taken three calls meant for Stephen. Stephen is extension 4199. I, Tyson," he again points to his chest, "am extension 4190."

Dick! I calm my thoughts before replying. It will do me no good to piss him off any further. "I apologize for the errors." I jot Stephen and Tyson's name on a sticky-note along with the correct extensions. "It won't happen again," I vow.

With no words, Tyson strides to the back office. A muscle in his is strong masculine jaw twitches as he avoids my gaze. Wow. The youngest Lennox has a giant chip on his shoulder. Dick. Ginormous. Egotistical. Prick.

Two calls later, I slowly transfer a call to Stephen's extension. As I sort outgoing mail into a Kansas City and other pile, Tyson storms through the heavy glass doors, aiming his steely gaze at me. If his eyes were lasers, I would disintegrate instantly.

"You just did it again," he howls.

With my voice stuck in my throat, I shake my head.

"I just answered my phone. It was a caller for Stephen," he claims.

"I just received a caller asking for Stephen, I pressed this button, right here." I point to the button labeled Stephen on the switchboard. "I am aware you stated his extension is 4199, but on my switchboard, all I do is press Stephen's name to transfer the call."

Tyson's face grows two shades redder. If this were a cartoon, steam would be escaping his ears. He pulls out his cell phone with great flourish. I have to look away as my phone begins to ring.

"Good morning, Lennox Law Firm, how may I direct your call?" I greet.

After an exasperated sigh he demands, "Transfer me to Stephen" He peers over the switchboard to witness my pressing the 'Stephen' button. Moments pass. "Fuck!" he shouts. With no explanation, he rounds the desk, and rolls my office chair with me on board out of his way. He proceeds to pull the plastic cover off Stephen's button and switch it with the 'Tyson' cover. He skirts the desk on his way once again to his office.

"Hold on," I demand. "Why..."

"Someone played a prank on you. Now you can transfer to the correct locations." His eyes never meet mine. He turns and retreats before I can say another word.

I sit dumbfounded. No 'I'm Sorry,' no 'forgive my tirade,'—Tyson Lennox just returns to the back office.

I leave the law firm promptly at one. I nibble on my brown bag lunch on the drive to the gym on Water Street. Oddly, I am more nervous to work at the gym than at the law firm. It is the unknown that scares me. What kind of work can a temp do at a gym? I guess I am about to find out.

When my phone announces I arrived at my destination, I am skeptical of the two-story, early 1900's design with big windows in the red-brick facade. The large, first-floor windows are blacked-out as is the glass door. A small, simple sign mounted above the door announces it is indeed Dempsey's Gym. Instead of the diagonal slots in front of the gym, I choose to park farther down the block.

I glance at the information sheet Gloria gave me. Unfortunately, it only gives me the address, name of the gym, and the owner's name. I look from the paper to the rectangular sign saying, 'Dempsey's Gym.' There is nothing fancy about it. As a female, this is not a gym I would ever join based on the exterior.

I pull the black door open. Immediately a waft of stale sweat invades my nostrils. I try hard not to show my repulsion as I need this job. Upon entering, I marvel that the gym encompasses two storefronts and extends even farther lengthwise. I make a note to inspect the second storefront after work this evening. My heels clomp loudly on the linoleum entryway. Trying not to draw attention, I tiptoe further.

"Just a minute!" A muffled yell comes through a mouthpiece from a boxing ring in the center of the space. Which of the two boxers said it, I cannot tell.

I tiptoe on the squishy mats closer to the ring. My hope to not draw attention failed. Roughly ten sets of eyes stare at me. Only the two sparring in the ring ignore me. I'm a fish out of the water. My morning job and my afternoon job are at opposite ends of the spectrum of work attire.

A loud buzzer sounds from near the ring. The two boxers separate while they strip off gloves and headgear. They expel their mouthpieces and begin commenting on each other's techniques. Both men shimmer in sweat from their wet hair to their shiny shins. A shaggy-haired blonde man approaches my side of the ring.

"Ms. Cochran, I presume," his deep male voice manages between gasps of breath.

"Yes, call me Ali," I reply. I offer my right hand to shake his but realize his arms are full of gloves, wraps, headgear, and a mouthpiece. I quickly retract my arm.

"Ali," he smiles at me once he exits the ropes and hops to the mat beside me. "I'm Clay. Why don't you take a seat in the office over there while I clean up a bit in the locker room before I join you." He motions with his head toward a window in the back corner with the words 'OFFICE' above it.

I stand frozen in place as I watch Clay saunter toward the locker room door just down from the office. The defined muscles in his sweat-slickened back flex with his every step. His silky boxer shorts, now damp, cling to his delicious glutes. He pauses to lean on the locker room door, his eyes catch mine. He smirks knowingly before disappearing inside.

Crap! My boss! My boss! He is my boss, and he just caught me checking him out. I am sure my jaw was on the floor, drool dripping over my chin, and my eyes were as wide as saucers when he caught me. I am oh-for-two on making a good impression on my first day on the job at these positions. *Focus Ali, focus.*

I tiptoe to the office, trying to clear my mind of the inappropriate thoughts I just had for Clay. I hope he returns in jeans and a button-down shirt, so I can focus on work for the afternoon. I search the wall inside the door for the light switch. As bright light engulfs the small office, an audible gasp escapes my lips.

It's an office, that much is true. Two black, metal file cabinets stand opposite the open door. One drawer tips open a bit with papers strewn this way and that upon the file folders inside. Most of the closed drawers have papers peeking out. Their tops contain shoe boxes full of documents. Next to the office door, under the large dusty window, sits the metal desk and office chair. The reddish-

brown leather of the chair is worn. A few tears repaired with gray tape decorate the seat and back—the entirety of both arms is covered in tape. I cringe as my eyes move to the desktop. I can conduct no work at this desk. More shoe boxes and desk trays heaped full of papers cover most of the top. Styrofoam coffee cups and fountain cups are scattered across the surface. Dust. An actual layer of visible gray-brown dust covers most of the piles. Heaven help me find the patience to complete this job. 'I need the money, I need the money,' I chant internally.

"So, where do we start?" Clay startles me from nearby in the door frame.

"Umm..." I search for a polite reply. "Why don't you tell me why you called the agency and what you'd like me to do for you."

He runs his thick fingers through his long layered blonde hair. The movement draws my attention to his broad shoulders and brutish biceps straining the stretchiness of his pale blue V-neck t-shirt. "Well, as you can tell I am not good at paperwork," he laughs. "I'm just like my grandfather was before me."

"Grandfather?" I ask my thoughts a muddled mess.

"Let's back up. Here, take a seat." He motions to the office chair. "I inherited this gym from my grandfather." He points to a black and white photo hanging behind the desk. I study the two young boxers battling in the ring. "Most of this mess was his, but the new layers are mine." He does have the decency to seem embarrassed by the state of the office. "In here we have six months of my paperwork along with over twenty years of my grandfather's."

Seriously? Over twenty years of receipts, documents, and invoices all thrown here or there. My mind boggles for a means of attacking the mess. Where should or can I start? Gloria will owe me big for this assignment. I make a mental note to document the office in pictures to show a before and after transformation. I mean, that is IF I'm able to work a miracle in here.

"Besides organizing the office, are there other tasks you would like me to do?" What am I thinking? It will take a year if not the rest of my life to organize this place.

"I need help setting up billing, invoices, etc. for the monthly membership dues. I need to create a budget of bills and income, so I might be able to start advertising or holding fights here." Clays eyes spark at these ideas.

"Okay." *Really? Am I agreeing to tackle this?*

"Umm, we are, um..." He struggles to find his words. "You are over-dressed for the gym. Maybe a shirt and jeans or shorts would be better. You can't come dressed like that, or the guys will be distracted by you. I don't need a boxer knocked out while eyeing you." His mouth quirks up on one side.

"Yeah, I came straight from a legal position this morning," I explain. "It was eating lunch or skip lunch to change clothes on my way here."

Clay nods. "You are welcome to change here. I don't want you to skip lunch and pass out on me or something." He chuckles. "I mean you'll need your strength to work through all of this." His arms spread wide to show the office, but my eyes admire his slim waistline in contrast to his muscular thighs and upper body. Damn! He's fine.

"Got it." I peek at a document in front of me and the one immediately under it. "I better get started," I hint.

"I'll be out on the floor. If you need me just holler." With that, he walks away.

Okay, sort and conquer is the plan. I toss the cups into a nearby trash can. I decide to start piles on the tile floor as it's the only available surface.

At five, Clay sticks his head in the door and announces it is time for me to call it a day. I sit back in the surprisingly comfortable office chair while I smile proudly at my progress. To others, it won't seem like much. To me, the three piles on the floor and two full trash bags outside the office door are my gold medal for a hard day's work.

"Everything go okay? Need anything on Thursday?" Clay asks, leaning his arm on the doorframe. It seems he purchases them a size smaller than needed. I see the stitching stretch at the giant biceps beneath. His pectorals and ab contours squeeze against its front.

"Can I bring a folding table and some boxes with me?" I inquire.

He scratches his stubble-covered chin. "I think I have a table and boxes upstairs in storage. I'll lug them down for you. If you want to work four or five days a week, feel free to come on in. The sooner I get organized, the sooner I can start new promotions."

"That would be great. I'll see you Thursday, then." I exit the office.

"Hey Ali," he calls after me. "I know it's a mess, but I can tell you made progress today." His sexy smile causes my breath to stall in my chest. All I can manage is a small wave before I escape.

Safe inside Gertrude, I text the office pictures to Gloria with a caption of 'The Gym. You owe me BIG. These are the before pics.' I close with a sticking-out-my-tongue emoji. I start Gertrude, desperately needing a glass of wine and a shower.

I settle for a glass of tap water and a warm bath while I dream of making enough money to reside in an apartment with a shower. In my daydream, I also drink wine while watching cable TV before turning in for the evening. Someday I will have these things again. Until then, I'll make due.

Jack: Did you box?
Ali: No, I'm dirty though
Jack: Sweat?
Ali: No, dust and grime
Ali: (I send the before pictures of the office)
Ali: This is my job. I get to organize years of paperwork and trash in the office.
Jack: Just toss it all
Ali: Can't. Must keep business records several years for taxes, etc.
Jack: I can see the dust
Ali: I know. I am covered in it.

Jack: Is the entire gym this messy?
Ali: No, just not into office work.
Jack: Do you like it as much at the law firm?
Ali: Today one of the lawyers was a huge dick to me.
Ali: It took everything I had not to tell him to fuck off.
Jack: What happened?
Ali: Call me, too much for a text

I answer Jack's call and proceed to share the entire story of the prank gone wrong today. He wants me to be careful around Tyson Lennox.

CHAPTER THREE

Ali:

Before I know it Friday arrives. Week one of my two placements is almost over.

"Hello," the female caller greets when I answer my next incoming call. "I know you are covering for Ray, what's your name?" her anxious voice inquires.

"My name is Ali. How may I help you?"

"I'm Stephen Lennox's wife, Marcia," the caller states. "There's been an emergency with our daughter, Laila. Stephen's at trial. I need to get a message to him that she broke her arm and hit her head. We are on our way to North Kansas City Hospital's E.R." She takes a shaky breath. "Can you give this message to his assistant, so she can tell Stephen if he calls during a break from the trial?"

"Marcia, I will. You drive carefully, take care of Laila, and we will get the message to Stephen." I console. I can't imagine the fear of a mother rushing her daughter to the E.R.

"Thank you." Marcia hangs up.

I buzz Stephen's assistant and leave a message for her to see me as soon as possible for an urgent message. I don't feel this is a message I should leave on her voicemail. I know she is at lunch. Maybe I can catch her as she returns.

I'm transferring a call to Marshall Lennox when the elevator dings and Tyson Lennox steps off. I wave, signaling I need to speak to him before he enters the back office. I try my best to ignore the look of disdain on his face. He makes it very clear that pausing a moment at my desk is the last thing he wants to do right now.

Once off the phone, I explain. "Marcia called, she needs to get a message to Stephen."

"He is in trial and can't be bothered," Tyson interrupts.

"She is aware, that is why she called here. Their daughter broke her arm and hit her head. They are on their way to The North KC E.R." I draw in a quick breath. "If Stephen calls in during the break, she wants us to let him know."

Tyson darts to the elevator. He presses the call button repeatedly. "Please, tell my assistant to reschedule my afternoon appointments. I will be at the hospital." The elevator doors open then close, carrying Tyson away.

The look of despair at the news of his niece's injuries will remain burned on my brain for weeks to come. This rude, intolerant man melted with fear for her. *Is this proof that this man has a heart?* I reserve my judgment until I gather more facts.

When my shift ends, I approach Stephen's assistant to ask if I can take up a collection to purchase a gift for his daughter. I learn that the office never sends flowers. I shrug and inform her I will do it on my own then.

"Wait," she orders while opening a locked drawer in her file cabinet under the desktop. "How much do you want?"

"Umm..." I pause to think.

"I'll give you sixty—it's for a good cause. Laila is a doll." She slides three twenties towards me. "It's petty cash. Please save your receipts."

"Will do. Thank you."

"I am sure they have left the E.R. by now, so here is Stephen's address." She slides a sticky-note my way. "Thank you for taking care of this. I need to make these calls, or I would offer to go."

I wave her off. Shopping with someone else's money to buy a gift for an eight-year-old girl, I can handle this. Before my relocation to Kansas City, I was an expert shopper with my parents' money. I miss shopping. My lack of money halted my shopping immediately.

After a long afternoon organizing the chaos of the office, Clay reaches his long arm around the corner flipping the lights off. Startled, I scream and the old office chair creaks as I scramble back to the corner in hopes of shielding myself from danger. I analyze the large figure through the doorway standing on the other side of the folding table blocking the door. The lights of the gym allow me to recognize it's Clay.

His holds the palms of his hands near his shoulders and apologizes profusely for scaring me. He claims his intention was only to turn the lights off and send me home for the weekend. He slides the folding table to the side careful not to disturb my organized stacks of papers and files. Flicking on the lights he enters the office.

I laugh as the fear fades and I replay my reaction in my head. *What was I so afraid of? Did I think a stack of invoices from 2006 were going to slice and dice me to death?*

"You've been busy." Clay states noticing only one stack remains on the corner of the desk. "I didn't know the desktop was real wood."

"Amazing what you'll find when you file papers instead of toss them on top of others over and over again." I tease.

"I've previously admitted my weaknesses. There's no need to beat a dead horse." Changing the subject, he continues. "Any plans tonight?"

I'm caught off guard. What are his intentions? I explain I need to run a get-well gift by for Laila Lennox from the staff at the firm by Stephen's house on my way home. Then my current novel will be calling my name. I ask if he has big plans for the weekend.

Clay shrugs, claiming just the usual hanging out and drinking beer. After hearing his words and observing his actions, I believe he wanted to hang with me tonight. My stomach flutters. My legs feel weak and my cheeks seem hot.

Get a grip Ali! What is going on with me? I am not a teenager swooning for every cute guy I see. I concentrate on my breathing in then out. I look away from the sexy Clay while I straighten up and grab my purse. "See you Monday. Have a great weekend." I offer as I exit the office and gym.

***

The Maps App instructs me onto Wildbriar Drive before it announces I arrived at my destination on the right. As my blinker ticks its rhythm, I marvel at the brick monstrosity. I grew up with two CPA's as parents. My home was nothing to sneeze at, but this house makes mine look small. Perhaps I should research the firm I work at daily. The Lennox Family must be vicious in the courtroom to earn this money.

With a gift bag in one hand, I nervously extend my empty one to press the doorbell. I smooth down my hair in anticipation of Stephen or Marcia answering the door. A gasp escapes at the sight of Tyson in their doorway. He's the last person I expect to answer the door.

His suit gone, Tyson stands in worn jeans and a white button-down with a blue collar and rolled up cuffs. His brown hair is messier than he wears it to the office, and it softens his normally stern appearance. Yum-yum. The butterflies migrate to my stomach and my heart threatens to pound a hole in my chest. My palms sweat, and my mouth is like the Mojavi Desert.

Odd that my body reacts to this version of Tyson and didn't to the office one. I did admire his handsomeness upon meeting him Monday. Perhaps his rudeness on Tuesday blinded me to all his attributes. This Friday evening, casual Tyson comes as a pleasant surprise. I refrain from fanning my face and collect my straying thoughts.

"Tyson, who is it?" Marcia calls from inside the house. At her words, Tyson snaps out of his statue-state.

"What brings you by?" He shakes his head. "I mean, hello. This is a surprise."

Raising the gift bag, I explain. "I bear gifts for the injured Laila from the entire staff." I extend the bag for him to take.

Having heard my words on her approach, Marcia pushes Tyson aside. "Aren't you thoughtful. Tyson, invite our guest inside." She swats his shoulder before disappearing.

As I begin to protest, Tyson motions me to enter. No words

between us, he is as shocked at my arrival as I am at his opening the door. I step inside then to the side for him to lead the way. I planned to drop the gift bag and head home, but I can't be rude to my bosses or one's wife. I reluctantly follow Tyson and vow I will quickly present the gifts then leave.

As we traverse the long foyer, my eyes devour his ass in the faded jeans and his strong shoulders in the snug shirt. Stop, I scold myself. Tyson is the same dick that flew into a rage when I sent his brother's calls to him on my first day alone. The same dick that didn't apologize when we uncovered it was the switchboard and not my fault. It was a cruel joke. *Why is a dick of epic proportions so hot? Not fair.*

"Who is her?" a small male voice asks Tyson while pointing at me.

"Hi, I'm Ali. I work with your daddy," I answer before Tyson can spout his typical rudeness toward the sweet boy.

"You work with Uncle Ty-thon and daddy?" the boy asks me with a cute lisp.

"Yes." I bend down to his eye level. "What is your name?"

"I'm Joe." He tugs me toward the kitchen. I chuckle as I allow him to pull me along. "Mommy," he calls using an outside voice.

"Ali?" Stephen smiles, looking at Tyson then me. I am sure his mind is full of questions.

"I'm delivering a gift for Laila from the office staff," I quickly inform the room.

"Really? That's sweet of you. Marcia, meet Ali. She's covering for Ray." Stephen's arm wraps Marcia tight to his side.

"It's nice to meet you in person," I greet.

"You didn't need to drive all the way out here," Marcia states. "Let's go see if Laila's still napping."

I follow Marcia to the family room. I hear footsteps behind me as the men follow. Joe sprints by all of us.

"LaiLai, look Uncle Ty-thon friend," he announces, pointing my direction once again.

I find myself wondering how often 'Uncle Ty-thon' brings female friends to meet his niece and nephew. *Stop.* It's none of my business. I can't spend my time fantasizing as if I'm in a romance novel. I gave up men when I left Hannibal. I remind myself I am focusing on me right now. I can't revert back to the old Ali. Fawning over men and dating must wait.

"Hi Laila, my name is Ali. I work with your dad at the office. I have gifts for you from everyone at the office." I smile down at the little girl as she rises from her pillow. I notice a slight wince as she positions a pillow under her cast to help hold its heavy weight. "Do you feel like opening a gift now, or should I have your dad take it to the kitchen for you to open tomorrow?" I tease.

"Now of course," she states as she extends her good arm toward the large gift bag.

I assume a spot on the sofa near Laila. I find Marcia, Stephen, and Tyson smiling at me. I wiggle uncomfortably, trying to focus my attention on Laila.

First, she pulls out the coloring book, next the markers with gel pens, and then squeals. "A diary!" She tucks it to her chest and looks up to me. "I've always wanted a diary!"

"Every young lady needs a diary," I state. I lean in using my hand to cover the distance between my mouth

and her ear. I whisper. "Be sure you hide your keys in two different places so that your parents and little brother will never find them."

Laila still clutches the floral diary to her chest. "I will, I promise." Then she motions for me to lean toward her. "I will put one under my mattress and one in my treasure box," she whispers.

I smile approvingly.

"What are you two whispering about?" Tyson asks, smiling. Dimples. The man is blessed with a cleft in his chin and dimples in his cheeks. It's just cruel.

"Nothing," Laila tells him, then smiles at me.

"You two are trouble," he states. "Stephen, I think we need to keep these girls apart. They are planning something," he teases.

"Dad," Laila sing-songs. "Tell Uncle Tyson to stop teasing me. I am in way too much pain to put up with it tonight." Her sad expression melts her father's heart.

"Tyson, take it easy. She's on pain meds and has a concussion," Stephen warns while Laila sticks her tongue out at Tyson, smiling.

Oh my, this girl is a pro at the age of eight—she knows how to work her dad to get her way.

"Laila, I'll stop teasing you and your new friend Ali if you tell me what the two of you are whispering about," Tyson promises.

Laila shakes her head his way. "Girls' Team, right Ali?" she taunts at Tyson.

The smile on Tyson's face melts all grievances I once had with this man. With his family, with these kids, Tyson is a different man. He teases. He plays. He smiles. He is relaxed. Gone is the uptight, hard-faced, litigator in an expensive suit. *Is this his element, or is the office?*

When the doorbell chimes, I claim I should be leaving. Laila and Joe immediately yell "no!" Marcia informs me the pizzas are here, and I should stay for dinner. I try to refuse, but Tyson tells me that Laila, in her

injured state, chose pizza for dinner, and they ordered more than enough for all of us. He rises from his armchair, tugs on my arm, and invites me to the kitchen to assist.

What can I do? Two of my bosses are here and insisting I stay for dinner. I walk with Tyson to the kitchen. We lay out paper plates, napkins, and water glasses on the island. Of course, Tyson instructs me here and there to find everything. I allow him to boss me only because he does so playfully. My days at the firm would be perfect if this Tyson showed up each day.

"Nothing better to do on a Friday night?" Tyson inquires.

"Even if I did, I would have brought the gifts. I broke my leg once. It is not fun being in pain and immobile. I had to try to make it toler-able for Laila."

Tyson shakes his head as a slight smile creeps upon his face. "But, you didn't know Marcia, you hadn't met Laila..."

"I had met her dad," I explain. "Marcia's voice on the phone today tore me up. I could feel her fear through the line. I thought of nothing else all day. I had to come."

"I'm glad you did. I don't know how you knew to buy a diary but judging from her reaction it was the best gift ever." He imitates Laila's clutching the diary to her chest. "You went above and beyond today. I'd do anything to take her pain away if I could. When I arrived at the E.R., she was crying in pain. Seeing her tears tore my heart out of my chest. All I could offer were words and hugs. I felt helpless."

I easily see pain upon his face. This man truly loves his niece. *Why hasn't some woman branded him with a wedding band and given him children already?* He's the father every woman dreams of for their future families. Well, at least this version of Tyson is.

"I have a soft spot for kids," I state, rescuing him from his emotion-filled confession. "I just bought items for

Laila that I liked at her age. She's starting to notice boys, so the diary is necessary to keep those secrets in."

"She is too young to notice boys," Tyson objects. "Stephen says she will date when she turns sixteen. I would wait until eighteen if she were my daughter."

I pat his arm as I greet Stephen and the pile of pizza boxes at the door to the kitchen. "I didn't say she is ready to date. She and her friends will be whispering about boys, spying on them at recess, and giggling about them. All of these secrets she will lock inside her diary." Stephen's eyes bug out of his head at the conversation he walks in on. "She needs a place to rant about her childish little brother and write about how 'Uncle Tyson' picks on her each day."

"Ali, give up," Stephen teases. "Tyson can't handle his niece and nephew growing older each day. If he had his way, they would remain in diapers and think he ruled the world, forever."

"I am awesome, and they know it," Tyson states. "You are their boring dad, and I am cool 'Uncle Tyson'."

"Don't you mean 'Uncle Ty-thon'?" Stephen corrects. We laugh.

"If you fix Laila's plate, I will carry it to her," I offer to Stephen.

"Smooth," Tyson teases elbowing me. "I need to step up my game if I want to compete with you."

"Whatever."

With plates of pizza and breadsticks, we settle around the family room. Marcia asks Laila what movie she wants tonight. When Laila chose Disney's *Mulan*, I know this little girl is my mini-me.

"That's my favorite movie," I announce. Looking at Laila, I explain. "When I was your age, everyone asked me who my favorite Disney princess was. I would always answer Mulan even though she wasn't a princess. She is awesome, loves her family, and can kick butt."

"It's Laila favorite movie, too," Joe adds. "We watch it all the time." He groans.

"Don't act like you don't like it," I respond. "My little brother loved it as much as I did. We would grab my mom's brooms and dance along with the soldiers."

"I don't dance," Joe states.

"It's not dancing." I stand. I place my plate of pizza on the coffee table and find a large, empty space on the floor to demonstrate. "Laila, will you sing with me?" I wait for her nod. "Let's get down to business," I pause so Laila will join in. "To defeat the Huns. Huu-ah!" I shoot my arms straight out in front of me as if I hold a wooden stake in them.

Joe rises beside me. With Laila's help, we sing and Huu-ah our imaginary sticks in the air.

"Okay you two, take a seat so we can start the movie," Tyson teases through his laughter.

Crap! I look from Tyson to Stephen. My bosses must think I'm crazy. Embarrassed, I return with head low to my seat.

"He's just jealous he doesn't know how to sing and do the soldier stuff," Laila whispers my way loudly.

Tyson, Stephen, and Marcia laugh out loud. Stephen collects himself. "I can't believe our luck." He looks at Tyson before his eyes return to me. "Ali, you're amazing at the firm. It feels as if you've been with us for years instead of a week. You went above and beyond with Laila's gifts. Now you're teaching my kids a dance for Laila's favorite movie. It's like you're part of the family." Tyson and Marcia nod in agreement.

"Shh! It's starting," Laila chides.

Thirty minutes into the movie, Laila and Joe are asleep on the sectional sofa. I help Marcia tidy up the remnants of the meal. Tyson and Stephen join us carrying on a conversation about court today. When Tyson attempts to toss the leftover two pieces of pizza into the garbage, I spring into action. I quickly place my hands below the slices but above the trashcan while I demand Tyson to freeze. I remove the slices and put them in the empty pizza box, I close the cardboard lid and pat the top securely shut on the counter.

"I love leftover pizza," I explain. "I will eat it for breakfast or lunch tomorrow." I hope I seem innocuous enough. I don't want to hint at my dire financial situation. I don't need their pity.

"You like cold pizza for breakfast?" Tyson restates with a smirk. I think he finds me interesting. I fear I have revealed too much about me this evening. Surrounded by family, I relaxed and let my guard down. *How will he treat at work now that he knows more about me?*

As I say my good-byes, Tyson hovers close to my side. "I'll walk you out," he states before he says his good-byes. "I'll swing by before lunch to entertain Laila," he informs his brother.

I cringe at the door, realizing Tyson will see Gertrude at the end of the driveway. Closing the door behind him, he places his hand on the small of my back to guide me down the walkway.

"Thanks again for dropping by tonight. You helped bring a smile to Laila's face." He kicks a pebble.

"You're welcome. I'll see you Monday. Have a great weekend." I don't wait for a reply. I walk toward my car.

"Ali," Tyson calls. As I turn to face him, he continues. "I'm sorry for the way I behaved this week. There's a lot on my plate, but you don't need to know that. I..." He runs his long fingers through his wavy, brown hair. "Just know I am sorry. You didn't deserve it."

Words fail me. I shrug it off, wave at Tyson, and dart to my car. My back still feels the warmth of his hand as we walked from the house. It is as if he still touches me, he is still with me. I don't allow myself to ponder the events of the night on the drive home. Once inside my tiny apartment, the floodgates burst. *What? How? What happened tonight?* I drove there to drop off a gift, not spend hours eating, playing, and chatting with two of my bosses. *How could Tyson act the way he did at the office then turn into such a relaxed and fun guy at night? Who is the real Tyson-- the dick or the hottie?*

I toss and turn, unable to turn my mind off to sleep. No matter how hard I try to remind myself this is a temporary position, Tyson is my boss, and I have to worry about money, not men... I can't let it go.

If I'm not thinking of Tyson, I am strategizing my tasks to maximize efficiency at Clay's gym. The man is not into paperwork or office work. I spent my first two days organizing the mayhem into piles. Next week I can begin working on one pile at a time.

Clay has a gift with clients. He enjoys working out and helping others work out, that much is clear. Membership dues, bills, and office work he avoids like the plague. As we discussed, I will work five days a week until I catch him up.

Tyson and Clay. Clay and Tyson. My bosses. I need to leave work at work. I need to get my head straightened out. I need to focus on taking care of me. I've come alive this week. I look forward to work—I actually am excited. I feel like a part of me is back.

Ali: So dick of a lawyer is not a dick

Ali: dropped get well gift to boss's daughter tonight, he was there since she's his niece

Ali: very different guy away from work

Jack: how?

Ali: kind, teases, caring, helpful

Jack: hmmm, Jeckyll and Hyde?

Ali: verdicts still out on that one

Jack: nice one

Ali: I need to talk the lingo if going to be at firm six weeks

Ali: He was someone I would enjoy hanging with tonight

Jack: your boss?

Ali: I don't plan on crossing any lines, but a girl can dream

Jack: This is where your little brother says goodnight

Ali: love ya

Jack: Love ya too

CHAPTER FOUR

Ali:

"Good morning Mr. Lennox," I greet.

"Ali, please call me Stephen. My father is Mr. Lennox." His smile proves his sincerity. "The kids couldn't stop talking about you this weekend. It was Ali this and Ali that. Uncle Tyson's friend Ali..." He chuckles.

"Laila and Joe are adorable. You know, if you ever need a sitter I'm your girl. I love to hang with kids." And I desperately need the money, I think to myself.

"I just might take you up on that," Stephen promises. "We attend many functions in the community for the firm and the high school age sitters Marcia finds scare me." He shudders. "I never know if they are stealing from us, in our liquor cabinet, ignoring the kids, or having their boyfriends over while we are out."

I only smile as the switchboard lights up with two incoming calls. Stephen approaches the glass doors as I wave. I hope he takes me seriously. I love to earn money while playing with kids. It rescues me from my quiet evenings and weekends. A social life would drain my funds...not that I have funds to waste.

I glance at today's digital calendar. Tyson isn't in court this morning. My insides warm, realizing I will see him soon. What a difference three days make. Friday morning, I woke thinking Tyson was a focused lawyer incapable of displaying any kindness. Today I woke anxious to see him again.

A grin graces my face as I recall how handsome Tyson was in casual clothes. Simply losing his suit jacket, removing the tie, and rolling up his sleeves transformed him into a laid-back hunk. Around his family, Tyson smiled, he chatted, he was playful, and he teased. He was the polar opposite of his work persona.

The ringing phone calls me back to my work. I smile at an approaching visitor as I answer. After the call I greet the client and inform them I will page Mr. Lennox. As I buzz Stephen's assistant informing him Mr. Lennox's 9:30 is here, Tyson exits the elevator. I prompt the client toward the glass doors as Tyson approaches my desk.

"What's up?" Tyson asks. I'm caught off guard by his casualness. He's in his navy suit with a pin-striped dress shirt and a vibrant tie, but he speaks like casual Tyson did Friday evening.

"Just a typical Monday morning at the reception desk." I reply as two phone lines ring in unison. Tyson pounds his fist twice on the desk, drawing my eyes back to him as I speak to the caller. He waves before disappearing into the back office.

Clay is not at the gym when I arrive. Instead a member I've seen most afternoons knocks on my office door moments after my arrival.

"Clay asked me to hang around this afternoon in case any members need something," he explains. "He asked me to tell you to text him if you need to and he'll try to call you later if he can." With his task complete he approaches the boxing ring and the two members sparring.

I want to ask if Clay is okay, if his family is okay and the reason for his not being here, but I doubt Clay gave him any answers. I also wonder why Clay didn't text or call to tell me he would be out today.

Mid-afternoon my cell vibrates on the wooden desktop. As I approach it from the file cabinet I'm working on today, I take pride in my conquering the mountainous piles that previously covered the desktop.

I have a text.

Clay: Sorry, family stuff today
Me: No prob, everything okay?
Clay: Nothing new, they needed my help
Me: ☺
Clay: how's the gym? I really need to get you a key to
the door
Me: Just normal afternoon, I'm tackling a file cabinet
Clay: Nice
Me: It may just be a drawer today, we'll see
Clay: Maybe only half drawer? ☺
Me: If my boss stops texting I should get through an
entire drawer
Clay: Bye then

I chew my thumbnail as I wait for another text. I'm glad to hear from him. My mind imagined many horrible scenarios that might pull him away from the gym he loves so much. Perhaps now I can fully focus on my tasks.

—————

Jack: Did you dream of Jeckyll or Hyde last night?
Ali: I wish
Jack: nightmare?
Ali: always

Jack: time to get professional help?
Ali: not yet
Jack: back to your boss
Ali: bosses
Jack: OMG both?
Ali: Nothing IRL
Jack: fantasies about your bosses are dangerous
Ali: I don't have cable, don't take them away from me
Jack: Okay
Jack: Start dating
Ali: My bosses? Really?
Jack: No other guys, go to clubs, whatever
Jack: get out and meet people
Jack: mad at me? Not going to reply?
Ali: I don't think I am ready for that
Jack: but you fantasize about bosses
Ali: that's harmless in my apartment
Ali: dating is in public, strangers, and people judging
Ali: not up for that yet
Jack: Okay, so I will let you dream of your bosses
Ali: thank you
Jack: If you had to pick today, which one would it be?
Ali: tough one
Ali: Clay is sexy in a surfer/skater boy that boxes kind of way
Jack: No using words like sexy. I am your brother.
Ali: Tyson is more the cute quiet type that you long to know what he's thinking
Jack: so pick one...
Ali: I can't. I know Clay better because he is easy-going at work.
Ali: Tyson is so professional at the office, that I've only caught a glimpse of his casual side.
Jack: sounds like Clay it is
Ali: Really?
Jack: so far. Got to go. Love ya.

Clay's hard body is firm to my back. As his hot breath brushes my neck, his arousal presses into my lower back. One arm wraps around the front of my shoulders while his other hand digs into my hip pulling me to him.

His warm mouth caresses my earlobe before he lightly nips. A low moan escapes and I rock my hips allowing his erection to grind against me. I want more. I need friction of my own. I entwine my fingers in his and encourage his hand from my hip over my abdomen, then down toward me center. I attempt to pull my hand away, but Clay keeps my fingers with his. We press together over the top of my shorts. I grind myself into our fingers. I find the fabulous friction coils my core tighter and tighter.

No! Don't stop! My eyes fly open. I pound my fists and attempt to kick my legs against my mattress. My legs are entwined in my sheet. Frustrated I groan. Beads of sweat cover my brow, I'm winded, and aroused. Very aroused.

I need water. I complete my escape from the sheets and head to the kitchen. As tap water fills my glass, I fan my overheated face. I open a window to cool my tiny apartment, before climbing back in bed.

I decide to read on my Kindle App as there is no way I will fall back to sleep right now. I struggle to find a comfortable position. My overstimulated lady parts crave attention. As I sit propped on pillows against the wall, I remind myself this dream is better than my nightmares.

I close my book realizing a steamy romance won't help my current situation. Having thoroughly cleaned the apartment over the weekend, I have nothing to do but lie in bed. I give up. Opening my top dresser drawer, I clutch my vibrator in hand then return to my bed

---

I'm finding my weeks fly by. I enjoy my tasks and the people I work with. I'm busier at the law firm and more challenged at the gym. I'm beginning to fear the end of my time with each.

"Don't make any plans for tomorrow after work." Clay says around the folding table blocking the office door. Holding his palms towards me, he continues. "No arguments. I'm treating you to dinner to thank you for putting up with this mess on a daily basis." He quirks his sly grin before disappearing into the men's locker room.

My heart flutters and my stomach flips. His smile and tousled hair make him so damn adorable. When romance authors speak of quaking knees, quivering loins, and sex-on-a-stick, they speak of Clay. I mentally reprimand myself to stop lusting after my boss...again.

If it wasn't for the stacks of paper on the office floor and the folding table blocking the door, I would follow him inside. 'Guys Only' doesn't scare me. *I can't go to dinner with him. Can I? I mean, bosses do take employees to dinner occasionally, right? Am I overthinking this?*

Payday. Today's my first payday since I began at the firm and gym. While sipping my morning diet pop for caffeine, I log into my banking app. I squeal at the sight of $382 deposited into my account from the temp agency for one week's work. I grab a notebook and pen to do my monthly budget.

Expenses:
Rent, Electric, Nat.Gas, Cell Phone, Car Gas, Car Ins
= $693 + Groceries??

Income:
Week1 $403, Week2 $480, Week3 $520, Week4 $520 = $1,923

I calculate and recalculate. I'm not convinced. I decide to err on the side of caution. I allow myself a full tank of gas and $100 for groceries this week. I need a check or two before I allow myself extras. I haven't spent $100 on a week's groceries, as I haven't had it to spare. My mind boggles at the possibilities. I can get more than bread, peanut butter, and jelly this week. The cautious side of me knows I need to try to save some for future months. I will be back to scraping by when the next four to six weeks are over.

CHAPTER FIVE

Ali:

"Where are you taking me?" I ask as Clay locks the gym front door.

I fiddle with Gertrude's keys standing on the sidewalk behind him. It's a beautiful spring day and will be a great night with its slight breeze.

"I thought we would head to Rock and Run." He states, turning to face me as he slips his keys into his pocket. "Put your keys away. I think we'll walk. It's only a few blocks." He looks to me for approval of this plan.

I smile and tuck my arm through his, signaling my willingness to join him on a walk. "As long as Rock and Run has fries, I'm in."

As we walk, he asks about my plans for the weekend. I share I have no plans, just laundry. He shakes his head at my answer and shares he will attend a dinner with his parents to celebrate his father's birthday tomorrow night.

Clay selects a table for two on the patio, and we order beers. I fiddle with my silverware and napkin nervously as he passes a menu to me. I quickly choose an 'adult grilled cheese' and fries to order, then set the menu aside. The waitress returns with two glasses of water, informing us our beers will arrive shortly.

"So, tell me about your parents." I prompt, desperately wanting to break the ice.

"My mom is a retired elementary school teacher. My dad boxed professionally, then managed fighters until he retired five years ago." Clay explains.

"So, your grandfather wasn't the only boxer in the family," I prompt.

"Ya, dad was a National Golden Gloves Amateur Boxer. Grandpa trained him in the gym." A proud smile graces Clay's face. "He boxed professionally for ten years then managed boxers for another fifteen."

"Did you get to see any of his professional bouts?"

"He traveled a lot while I was young. Mom attended every fight, but I only saw three fights before he retired."

Our beers arrive. Before I take my first sip, I ask, "Will your dad's party be a big affair?"

Clay takes a long pull from his beer then places it on the table. His eyes glued to his amber ale, he answers. "No, it will just be mom, dad, my sister, and me." He traces patterns in the moisture collecting on the outside of his mug. "Dad struggles with memory issues some- times." His eyes glance my way before returning to his mug. "We try to keep things simple in case he's having a bad day."

"My grandmother suffered from Alzheimer's before she passed away." I offer sympathetically.

"Um," Clay finally looks to me as he speaks. "Dad's been diagnosed with symptoms of CTE."

"Oh!" It escapes before I can control it, so I attempt to cover my reaction. "I've read about CTE with NFL players. I hadn't thought about it affecting boxers, too. That sucks. I'm sorry." I reach across the table, patting his hand with mine.

"Yeah, 'sucks' is a good word for it." Clay smirks.

"Is this why you were gone on Monday?" I pry.

Clay nods. "Sometimes he's more than my mom can handle. When he's confused sometimes his anger spirals out of control." He shrugs. "He hasn't hurt anyone, but he destroys things around the house or puts holes in the wall. That's the reason my parents insisted I couldn't competitively box when I quit school to take over the gym."

"Your parents aren't happy you took over the gym?" I ask, wanting to know more.

"When grandpa died, my parents planned to sell the gym. It broke my heart to think of the gym that my grandfather and father spent so much of their lives in wouldn't remain in the family. The only way to save it was for me to drop out of college and take it over. After the shock of me leaving law school wore off, my parents realized how important it was to me that I keep the gym. They included a clause in the transfer of ownership that stated I could not compete as a fighter but could train and own the gym." Still fiddling with condensation on his mug, he glances up at me.

"Did you want to compete?"

"It's not something I ever considered. It might have been something I worked my way up to the longer I was here, but I agreed to keep my parents happy." He clears his throat. "Enough about me, how did you arrive in KC at the temp agency?" It catches me off guard when Clay shifts the conversation from him to me.

I quickly scramble for an honest answer I can share with him. "I struggled with my classes spring my junior year, so I dropped out, disappointed my parents, and drove to KC to start on my own." I only share part of the story, but it's the truth. I bite my lips together as I look toward the door. I contemplate a reason to leave, if Clay presses for details.

Sensing I've shared all I intend to, he lifts his mug towards mine. "Here's to college dropouts killing it in KC."

I clink my mug with his. "I don't know that I'm killing it, but we seem to be making it work." I correct.

We give our food orders with our waitress. Clay orders us more beer, too.

"Thanks for joining me tonight." He says. "I can't tell you how much having you at the gym, working in the office has meant to me."

"Well, it's my job, and you pay me to do it." I remind him.

"I know it is, but it takes a special person to take on the mess I had." He responds. "I've been able to focus on the gym and training instead of feeling shackled to the desk." He chuckles. "The invoice program you selected seems easy enough even I can understand it, and the filing system you are implementing makes sense."

"When I get the last of the paperwork filed next week, I'll be able to transfer to the membership program and take over the invoicing for you." I offer.

Our fresh drinks arrive. Clay immediately proposes another toast. "To the

perfect person, at the perfect time, with the perfect skills to get the job done." We clink mugs and sip.

When our food arrives, our conversation takes on lighter tones. I enjoy my casual dinner with my boss. Clay walks me to my car, makes sure it starts, then waves good-bye before walking to his car.

Ali: Clay took me out to eat to thank me for working in messy office all week.
Jack: Date?
Ali: No, boss treating employee to meal.
Jack: Beer involved?
Ali: Yes
Jack: sounds like a date
Ali: Stop. It was nice. I learned about his family, the gym...it was nice.
Jack: nice?
Ali: Not a date. More like colleagues or friends
Jack: Friends would be good. You need those
Ali: How is baseball going?

Our conversation continues, but I can't help but analyze date vs dinner.

As I lie in bed, I think how easy it is to hang with Clay or Tyson away from work. We interact as friends. The line between boss and temporary employee continues to blur. I realize I should cease any interactions outside of work. Maybe Tyson and Clay want to spend time with me. Maybe they want to be my friend. I just need to remind myself to stop reacting like a sex-starved shut-in. Friends, I need to remind myself we can be friends. However, I can still hope for more.

CHAPTER SIX

Ali:

"Are you sure you are ready for this?" Stephen greets when he opens his front door.

"Ali's here!" Laila yells as she runs towards me. She wraps her arm and cast around my thighs in a tight hug.

"Careful," I remind Laila gently sliding her cast from my leg.

Stephen prompts Laila to allow me to enter the house.

"Bye Mom, bye Dad," Laila calls, entwining her hand in mine.

"Nice," Marcia chides. "Kids, go to the family room while we go over a few things with Ali." A few moans escape, but both scurry to the living room.

Marcia points out a notebook she keeps for sitters. All vital cell and emergency numbers are in it along with allergy information and medical consent to treat forms. She is easily the most prepared mother I've ever worked for. I escort them to the door, while ensuring I have everything under control here.

No sooner does the door latch and lock than the children begin chanting 'they're gone.' I laugh at their song and dance. "What should we do first?" I ask.

They rattle off we have movies to watch, games to play, snacks to eat, and costumes to try on before the parents return. I encourage each to name one thing, then we will flip a coin to see which we will do first. They have already eaten dinner, so snacks need to wait awhile. Joe chooses Wii Bowling and wins the coin toss. We bowl two games. Joe defeats both Laila and me. We laugh so hard the entire game that my sides ache.

Laila chooses to play dress-up. When she hands me a red cape and tiara I inform her I will just watch as the two of them play.

"Her game, her rules," Joe states matter-of-factly. It seems this family institutes rules during play time.

I swing my cape over my shoulders with a grand flourish before securing it at my neck. I allow Joe to place my crown upon my head. It has been quite some time since I last wore a costume, but I decide to make the most of it.

Joe wears a Hercules costume. Laila states it looks like a knight's costume. She dresses head-to-toe in princess attire—all of her pieces match perfectly. I balk when she requests we play with makeup. I'm no stranger to kids trying to break the rules while parents are out. I'm sure Marcia's makeup is off limits.

"I'll put it on Ali first, then Joe," Laila instructs.

As I prepare to disappoint her, I notice she holds play makeup in her little hands. Laila's name highlighted with tiny floral stickers is on the outside of the cases. I do not fight my fate. I assume my position on the small play chair, trying not to cringe at how bad this is going to turn out. To ensure Laila's face resembles our clown-like ones I suggest a makeup team effort for her. Joe and I take turns applying her makeup.

We place Laila's tea party set on the little wooden table. She instructs me on how to pretend that we have tea and cakes to eat. She explains Marcia doesn't allow them to use real drinks or snacks. She places a stuffed bear in the empty between Joe and me then her life-size doll in the chair next to her before she begins serving our tea.

I startle at the sound of the front doorbell. Marcia and Stephen didn't mention expecting company. I instruct the kids to stay in the playroom. They only argue for a minute but surrender when I firm my tone repeating my words. I pull my phone from my back pocket and unlock it in case I need to call for help. I quickly make my way to the top of the staircase then freeze in my tracks.

I hear heavy footsteps on the tile downstairs. I know I locked the front door. My heart beats double time at the realization it's an intruder. I glance to ensure the children haven't left the playroom before I descend the stairs, hugging the wall while I go. I hear noises in the kitchen—there goes my plan to grab a knife for protection. My brain scrambles for other possible weapons. In the family room, two wooden bats hang on the wall. As quietly as possible I make my way in, grab a bat, then position myself at the base of the stairs. I need to prevent the intruder from finding the children. I glance up ensuring the door to the playroom remains closed.

"Hey." A laughing male voice slices through the silence.

I quickly turn around. I cock my arms back in preparation to defend myself as my eyes focus on the intruder in front of me. Tyson? Tyson Lennox stands in front of me with a bag of chips and a jar of dip. His empty hand attempts to cover his smile, but his laughing eyes betray him.

"What the FUCK are you doing here!" I yell, my adrenaline and fear getting the best of me. My trembling arms lower the bat.

"Laila asked me to stop by tonight while you were here," he replies from behind his hand. Tyson's eyes twinkle as he continues to laugh.

"Here." I pass the bat to him and dart up the stairs. I can't let the children live another minute in fear of where I am. Outside the door, I announce, "It's okay, Tyson is here." Then I open the playroom door.

I find the two had continued the tea party without me. A stuffed bunny sits in my chair with a tiara between its ears.

"What have we here?" Tyson asks behind me. He stands close without touching me, yet I can feel the heat emanating off of him. The hair on the back of my neck prickles at his closeness.

Behave. My body's reaction to Tyson is unlike anything I've experienced before. I lose all control. Even as I chant to keep calm, control my breathing, and keep my thoughts rated-PG, my attempts fail miserably.

"I knew you'd come," Joe cheers.

It seems Laila and Joe plotted to get Tyson here and kept it from their parents and me. Tyson high-fives the two for their smooth plan. Instead of cheering, I worry. I hope these two don't think Tyson and I are a couple. They might get their hopes up. I need to nip this in the butt.

"Guys," I begin. "Your uncle and I work together."

"Duh," Joe replies.

"Tyson, do you like Ali?" Laila immediately asks. Tyson nods, trying to hide a smirk, but I see the corner of his lips twitch. I glare at him.

"Ali, do you like Tyson?" She looks at me, and I nod. "So, then you are friends," Laila proudly announces while folding her arms across her pink princess dress.

"Duh, friends that work together," Joe adds smugly.

The world according to a six and eight-year-old seems simple when stated that way. If only my adult world could be this easy. I miss easy.

"You started the tea party without me!" Tyson acts upset.

Joe quickly suggests a cape and party hat for Tyson to wear. Laila empties two chairs for us adults. Then she announces to him that her mom doesn't allow food or drink at the tea party. Tyson places his snack on the dresser top and assumes his seat as I take mine. When Laila tries to apply makeup, Tyson firmly refuses.

"You can't attend the tea party without makeup," I announce as I point at the three of us. "I'll apply yours and only use one item," I promise. Tyson's eyes squint as he tries to assess his trust in me. Laila and Joe chant 'do it' loudly while circling the table. Tyson gives in.

I decide guy-liner is all this prince needs to complete his look. My girl parts tingle at the thought of guy-liner. I love, love, love a guy in eyeliner: rockers, actors, and bad boys alike. I fight my quickening breath as I take the black eyeshadow in one hand and an application wand in my other. I ask him to close his eyes before I turn around. Perhaps then he won't see how worked up I am right in front of him.

I gently and quickly apply a thin black line on his lids along his upper eyelashes. I instruct him to open his eyes and next smudge thin lines below his lower lashes. I then ask him to lightly close his eyes again and I blow on both eyes to remove stray dust.

As I step back, his eyes open. Focused on me, I witness his pupils swell. His brown irises pierce me and his nostrils flare infinitesimally. Locked in his heated gaze, my breath stutters. I clumsily fumble my hands on the back of my chair before I lower myself for fear my legs might buckle at any moment.

Tyson breaks our gaze. "How do I look?" He asks Laila, then Joe. Laila giggles. Joe gives him a thumbs-up.

Tyson looks back to me and winks. Winks. His freshly lined eyes crinkle, and his mouth smirks. Heaven help me. I am way out of my league here. Even a six and eight-year-old outmaneuver me tonight. I need to gain back my control.

"Ten more minutes until movie time," I announce. "Let's wrap up our tea party and clean up for the movie." There. I again am the babysitter in control of the evening.

When Tyson suggests the guys clean up the playroom while the ladies prep the snacks it seems like a great plan, so I go along with it. Laila leads me by the hand toward the stairs and kitchen. I love how she prances in her princess costume. Laila is beautiful and confident— I hope she never loses her confidence.

When Laila and I enter the family room with popcorn, cookies, milk, and water; the guys are on the sectional ready for a movie. We place the snacks on the coffee table for all to reach. Laila cuddles in on the right side of Tyson, propping her cast on the arm of the sectional. I plop into the remaining spot between Tyson and Joe.

"What movie should we watch?" I ask, hoping not to cause a battle between the children.

"Uncle Ty-thon already put one in," Joe confesses.

Laila peeks around Tyson to me with wide eyes. It seems she doesn't trust him to choose an appropriate movie for all of us. Tyson presses play on the remote before laying it on the table.

As the opening credits roll on the large flat screen, Tyson excuses himself to fix an adult drink. Laila asks Joe in a whisper what movie Tyson chose. Joe shrugs. Upon hearing the first two notes, all three of us know what movie. We begin singing along with the opening of Disney's *The Lion King*. Tyson chose a favorite.

Upon his return, Tyson clinks his open bottle of beer against my water. After sipping, I place my water on a coaster and set the popcorn bowl in the open space between Tyson and me. We munch on the popcorn and finish our drinks as the kids fall asleep early in the movie. Tyson carries Laila as I carry Joe up to their bedrooms.

On our descent, Tyson states he will grab us two more beers while I find something to watch on television. I ask him to bring me a water instead. I nibble on popcorn, awaiting his return. I hope he will be okay with finishing the movie we started with the kids.

"You should probably take off the tiara, cape, and makeup before Stephen and Marcia return," Tyson suggests as he returns to the family room. I remove the cape then tiara, placing them on the bottom of the staircase. I note Tyson removed his costume but hasn't removed the eye makeup, so I leave my makeup intact. How he can look at me without laughing, I have no idea. Laila needs a lot of practice on makeup application before high school.

"Can you believe those two played the two of us and their parents?" Tyson asks. "I've always known they have me wrapped around their fingers, but to not tell you, Marcia, or Stephen took balls. Imagine what the teenage years might be like if they are this advanced already." He shakes his head as he chuckles. We sit silently as the movie plays. Finally, Tyson speaks. "I had fun tonight."

"Me, too," I confess before filling my mouth with a handful of popcorn and rinsing it down with a sip from my water bottle.

"You are so good with the kids; do you have younger siblings?" He asks.

I tell him I only have a brother, four years younger than me. I explain about my many years of babysitting, working as a lifeguard, and working at summer camps. When I point out he is the super-awesome Uncle Tyson in their eyes; he claims was easy to swoop in, give them what they want, then leave them with their parents. I correct him by explaining I don't believe that is how he feels at all. He shrugs.

The silence between us grows unbearable. I rack my brain for anything we have in common. All I come up with are questions. Is he a dog or a cat person? What's his favorite movie? What's his favorite food? What's his favorite thing to do away from work? I realize I can't interrogate him, so I ask a question that might lead to a conversation. "Tell me something most people don't know about you."

Without looking my way, he states, "I never wanted to be in the family business." Eyes still locked on the movie, he asks the same of me.

"I dropped out of college spring of my junior year." I will my gaze to stay on my twiddling thumbs in my lap. I shouldn't have shared this. He is my boss. A college drop-out is not the type to work at a legal firm. He will think less of me. Everyone does when they hear I'm a dropout. I hope he doesn't ask why I dropped out. It's a story I just can't share.

Silence again encompasses us. I fiddle with my empty water bottle. Tyson presses pause on the remote. I'm no longer in the mood for a Disney movie. Our statements weigh heavy on each of us. Several long, silent moments pass.

"Would you like another?" Tyson asks as he pulls my empty bottle from my hands. I stand and follow him. I walk to the kitchen with the remnants of our earlier snacks. Tyson quickly rescues a couple of items from my overloaded arms. Marcia and Stephen step in from the garage while we straighten up.

"I won't even ask." Stephen laughs taking in our faces.

"Looks like you played dress-up tonight," Marcia states also laughing. "Why does Tyson's face look so much better than yours?"

I explain his stubbornness and our compromise. Both adults laugh harder.

"Wait," Stephen interjects. "Why are you here?" He asks, pointing at his brother.

Tyson explains the creativity of the children in arranging a visitor without informing any adults. He warns Stephen he will have his hands full with Laila when she is a teenager since she can already pull the wool over her parents' eyes like a pro.

Marcia asks how everything went. I give a brief replay of our evening and tell her the children were on their best behavior. Stephen slips me cash while Marcia asks if I might be willing to sit again in the future.

"Of course," I reply quickly. I cringe, hoping they don't see how desperate I am to earn cash.

"I should be going, too," Tyson states. "I'll walk Ali out."

As I smile and wave, his large, hot hand finds its way to my lower back. I struggle to mask the gasp that escapes at his touch. On my way to the front door, warmth spreads from his heated palm over my entire body. A warmth of comfort, a warmth I haven't felt in nearly a year.

"Remember to go straight home."

"Pardon?" His comment confuses me. *Is he ordering me? Will he worry? Why does he care?*

"I mean because of Laila's makeup." He points to my face nervously. "I wouldn't want you to forget about it. You might get some stares at the store."

I forgot. I thank Tyson for reminding me. "Have a great weekend. I'll see you Monday morning." I scurry into my driver's seat and pull from the curb.

I distractedly drive from the prominent neighborhood back to my older residential area behind a strip mall. Thoughts of Tyson and the kids keep me occupied all the way home.

As I prep for bed, I ponder his confession. *Did Tyson not want to work at the same firm as his family? Did he want to practice a different type of law? Or did he not want to be a lawyer?* Judging by his reaction after making the statement, I doubt I will ever learn the meaning. It is obvious he didn't want to tell me.

CHAPTER SEVEN

Ali:

I'm slick and red. Everywhere I touch turns crimson. I'm back in our dorm room, and Leslie sits against her bed, surrounded by a puddle of blood. As I stare, her eyes open, and she motions for me to walk to her.

"Ali, I love you," she cries. "Ali, I only want to be with you."

She's still alive. I cradle her in my arms, attempting to carry her to my car. There's no time to call an ambulance; I can drive her faster myself. I move her into the elevator. When the doors close, we fall to the floor.

Leslie's eyes close, she's not breathing. I call to her over and over. She was just awake. I need her awake again. I can save her. I need to save her.

A distant siren calls me back to reality. My eyes open to the dark apartment. I climb from my bed for water. My body is covered in sweat, and my scalp and hair are damp. As I pad to the sink, I twist my head left then right to pop my neck and release tension. As water from the faucet fills my glass, I attempt to even out my breathing.

The nightmares still occur. The dark circles under my eyes prove they disrupt my sleep nightly. I need to purchase more concealer soon if I can't control the dreams.

"Hi." A familiar male voice greets me as I walk through the gym toward the office. I look up from my cell phone to find Tyson at a speed bag.

"Um," I mumble. "You're here at Clay's gym." I can't hide my shock as I stand frozen with my mouth agape. *Why isn't he at the office?* I mentally attempt to check the firm's schedule from this morning. I don't remember Tyson's afternoon schedule. "Are you stalking me?" I blurt out only partially teasing.

"This is my gym," he states matter-of-factly. I want to swat the smirk from his slight-stubble-lined face.

"Did you know this is the gym I worked at in the afternoons?" I wonder aloud.

Tyson nods. "Clay and I were in law school together. I joined the gym when he took it over." The irony in his words startles me.

This is just my luck. I get a call to come to the agency for not one job but two. The hours of each work perfectly for my schedule. I find myself becoming a friend with my boss at each position, only to find out they are friends. Both of my bosses are hot hunks that I now fantasize about. I find my thoughts straying to dreams that cause my cheeks to blush when in their presence. Knowing how my body reacts in the presence of one guy causes me to fear its reaction when I'm with both of them. I'm not sure I'm ready for that.

I feel like a character in the contemporary romance novels I read in between the self-help books from the library. I'm not naïve enough to believe this will all remain easy and smooth. No, my two worlds are about to blow up in my face—nothing this comfortable can ever work out for me.

I can't speak. I merely wave at Tyson as I retreat to the protection the office will provide. But, I'm not as protected as I hope. As I sit at the desk, I can see Tyson working out through the window. I scold myself for spending an hour scrubbing the office window clean last week. He removes his sweat-drenched shirt, revealing his defined back which glistens in the fluorescent lights from above. I am hypnotized by the sight of his muscles while he works the speed bag like a pro.

I need to focus on work. I cannot be side-tracked by Tyson in all his glory. I pull the string to lower the mini blinds over the large window. As would be my luck, the entire contraption falls from the brackets onto the desk, causing quite a raucous. All eyes in the gym turn on me as I struggle to remove the noisy blinds and place them in the trash can.

My Friday finds me playing with Laila and Joe again. This time Tyson overheard Stephen and I chatting at the firm, and he later informed me he might drop by. We play board games for hours before tucking the children in bed for the night.

I decide I need answers tonight. I ponder our previous conversation and his true meaning. "When you said you didn't want to be in the family business," I notice his stiff posture and tight jaw, "What did you mean?" I'm not sure he will open up to me.

Tyson leans forward, resting his elbows on his parted knees with hands clasped. "I didn't want to be a lawyer." His words spew from his lips. He doesn't sit back up or look my way. I sense he's uncomfortable opening up to me.

I clear my throat before I continue my inquisition. "What did you want to be?"

As much as I want an answer, witnessing his fidgeting while wringing his hands coaxes me to withdraw the question. Before I can speak, he does.

"I wanted to teach History." He turns to face me. "High school History."

I have to ask. "Your parents wouldn't let you?"

"I never asked," he confesses. "Everyone assumed I'd become a lawyer. So, I became a lawyer." He shrugs.

I marvel at the fact he never asked, he never hinted, he never confessed to the ones he loved his desire. He endured law school and passed the bar to do as others wanted.

"I couldn't disappoint them. I couldn't be the one to choose differently." I see the anguish in his eyes and on his face. Perhaps this is why he's a different person at work versus at home. "I just couldn't. I'm not as strong as Clay or you. I can't stand up to my parents. I couldn't break the mold of what they expected of me."

I place one finger upon his lips, silencing his words. "I believe you are stronger than you think you are. The Tyson I know is strong, caring, and loves children." I smile.

He attempts to smile back. My words do not convince him of the strength everyone else sees inside. My first impressions of him were not the real Tyson. I fear no one knows the real man, not even him.

"I'm worried the kids have the wrong idea about us," I tell Tyson on my way to Gertrude. The warm evening breeze tickles my bare arms.

"Why is that?"

"It seems they think you must visit every time I babysit. Stephen and Marcia don't need to pay me if you are here," I inform him, opening my driver's door. It creaks loudly, protesting the movement.

"I get to kill two birds with one stone," he replies. "I see Laila and Joe while enjoying time with you."

Don't read into that. Don't read into that. I tell myself. Too late. A shiver creeps from head to toe at the thought of Tyson enjoying time with me outside the office. I awkwardly wave good-bye and duck into my car. I need to escape. Gertrude refuses to make a noise when I turn the key. "Please don't do this now," I plead as I try the ignition two more times to no avail.

I jump in my seat at Tyson's knock on my window. "Trouble?" He asks, already knowing the answer.

I open my door. "Gertrude does this from time to time." I shrug. "She'll start tomorrow. I'll get an Uber." I nervously scroll through my apps.

"I'll drive you home." Tyson offers.

He can't see where I live. It's bad enough he saw Gertrude and now knows she is unreliable, I can't allow him to escort me home. "I'll be okay. Don't worry." I finish requesting my ride. "All done. My Uber will be here in three minutes."

Tyson shakes his head in frustration. "It's okay to let others help you from time to time. It's what friends do."

Friends. He thinks of me as his friend. He enjoys spending time with me as a friend. I officially need to rein in my out of control hormones. We are friends. I need friends in KC. *Will he ever think of me as more?* I rebuke my errant thoughts. "Thank you for the offer; I don't want to be a burden."

Tyson waits with me by Gertrude until my ride arrives. He opens the back door for me and says goodnight. I stifle a chuckle at the glare he shoots at my Uber driver. Like fear of Tyson will prevent any misconduct on his part. Men and their egos—how do they walk around with those things day in and day out?

CHAPTER EIGHT

Tyson:

"We should call Ali and ask her to join us tonight," Clay grunts, throwing punches to my ribs Saturday afternoon.

"You forget one thing," I counter between jabs at Clay. "We don't have her number."

Clay steps to the ropes, drinks from his water bottle, then states, "I have her cell. We could text our plans and invite her to meet us."

Clay's words strike me like an unblocked right uppercut to the chin. I can't believe she gave Clay her cell number.

"Dude," Clay removes his mouthpiece, and after our many years of friendship senses the turmoil swirling inside my muddled brain. "I don't always open the gym in the afternoon. On her first day here, I asked how to reach her if I wasn't going to be here to unlock the front door. Purely professional, I promise." He crosses his heart with his fingers.

"We done?" I spit. My mind fights the urge to kick his ass.

"Yeah, we're done," Clay confirms.

After showering, Clay decides to readdress the topic of Ali. "We need to figure this out," He says. "Our ten years of friendship is too important to ruin."

I know he feels something for Ali, and he now has confirmation that I do as well. This might be the true test of our friendship.

"Should we draw straws, place a bet, let her decide, or fight it out?" Clay grins, teasing.

I sit on the locker room bench, jeans on and shirt in my hands. Ever the analytical one, I try to process the best outcome for all three of us.

"Well, I refuse to fight you over Ali. So, we either agree on a plan going forward, or I step aside." I shake my head. "We don't even know if she wants to see either of us. I sense being her boss is a huge hurdle for her."

"So, maybe we should take her out with us tonight, watch her, and see if she seems into one or both of us. Then we can decide what to do," Clay offers.

I grin. "So, you are proposing we experiment with her feelings?"

"I'm not suggesting we force her hand or sway her decision in any way," Clay explains.

"Okay, text her."

Clay: Tyson and I are hanging at Rock and Run tonight, want to join us?

We continue to dress while we await her reply.

She takes too long to respond.

Clay: say yes
Ali: yes
Clay: will pick you up at 6
Ali: ☺

"Done," Clay states. "We are picking her up at six."

"She said yes?" I can't believe it. Clay slides his phone over for me to read the text messages.

"Well then, I'll pick you up at 5:45," I state. "Do you know where she lives?" I inwardly cringe, unsure I want to know how close he already is to Ali.

"I have no idea," Clay responds. "Surely it is on her information form the temp agency emailed us. Right?"

"Okay," I admit "I followed her home from Stephen's one night to make sure her beat up car got her home safely. Text her for the address. I don't want her to worry how we already know it."

Clay: Send me address
Ali: I can meet you there. No need to go out of way.
Clay: Picking you up. Holding you hostage until we want to take you home. So, send address.
Ali: Eastwood Lane, I'll be outside

"Got it," Clay boasts.

CHAPTER NINE

Ali:

I nervously tug my navy baby-doll top over the waistline of my shorts. I blow out a deep breath. Both. I'm going to be with both Tyson and Clay outside of work.

Clay's easy-going style relaxes me. I tend to let my guard down and have fun in his presence. I'm not sure if his playful teasing is just that or if he is flirting with me. I want to run my fingers through his tousled blonde locks while he kisses me senseless.

Tyson, on the other hand, exudes confidence in all he does. His sexy smile with delectable dimples dampens my panties every time.

I turn this way then that in my full-length mirror, hoping I look casual and calm. My insides are churning like river rapids. Clay's teasing acts like foreplay on my body. Put that with Tyson's superpowered smile, I'm sure to be a blubbering, aroused mess all evening. *Why did I agree to go out?* I should have responded no to Clay's text. *Please, please, please let me not make a fool of myself tonight.*

My cell phone alarm alerts me I should head outside so I'll be ready when they arrive. I check my cross-body bag, ensuring my ID and debit card are inside. I slip my phone in a pocket of the purse, lock my door, and descend my stairs to the street below. As I round the corner from my street to Eastwood Lane, I notice the men are parked halfway down the block.

"Hey guys," I greet, voice raised to reach them as they stand beside a sleek black GMC Denali. The Alpha male testosterone slaps me in the face as I approach. My nerves shoot to supernova strength.

"Before I climb in," I tease. "You're not going to murder me, cut me up into pieces, and distribute me to dumpsters all over Kansas City tonight, are you?" The guys chuckle. "Well?" I taunt.

"Just get in," Clay orders.

Safely secured inside, Tyson transports us toward our destination downtown.

As Tyson parks, he recommends I leave my purse in his car. "I can carry your driver's license for you, and you won't have to worry about it all night."

I realize I am only twenty-two-years-old and not the most social of daters, but I've never heard of a guy offering to carry items for a girl so she doesn't need her purse. Usually, women must beg them to do it. Wow. He is thoughtful.

"I could carry your cell in my pocket if you don't have one," Clay quickly chimes in, not to be outdone.

I chuckle at their offers. "Do either of you have room in your pockets for my tampons?" Both turn to face me over the center console with wide eyes and jaws open. Neither knows how to respond to me. I start to feel sorry for ruining a very thoughtful gesture with my little joke. "I'm teasing," I promise. "I will take you up on the offer to carry my license and phone." They relax a smidgeon. "Can you carry my debit card, too?" I ask Tyson.

Almost in unison, they make it very clear I will not need any money this evening. They are such gentlemen. I smugly pass my ID to Tyson and my cell to Clay as we head for the door of Rock and Run.

We sit on the patio, share appetizers, and drink beer. Our conversation flows easily.

After two rounds, Clay asks me to dance. There is no dance floor, and no one is dancing. An Imagine Dragons song finishes as we stand near our table. Our bodies begin to sway to the beats of Maroon 5. As the hits keep playing, we keep dancing, and a few other patrons join us. I notice Tyson entertaining himself on his phone as we continue to dance mere feet away. Four songs pass before Tyson asks to cut in on Clay.

Crap! An eighties power-ballad begins. This means Tyson and I are dancing to a slow song. I nervously sway with him, trying to keep an appropriate boss/employee distance between us. Although we seem very comfortable in each other's arms, I am not sure if the chemistry flows both ways. He tosses around the word friend, while I melt into a puddle near him. Maybe I am the only one feeling the connection.

Next, the speakers play "Sit Still, Look Pretty" by Daya. I am grateful to step away from Tyson to try to gain my composure. I lose track of songs by the time Clay approaches.

"I think you need to take this." Clay extends my cell phone towards me. "This Jack-guy seems to be getting upset you aren't answering his texts."

Do I detect jealousy in his words? It isn't anger. I grasp my phone while I head for our table. As I scroll through eight texts from my brother, I snicker at his growing concern.

Jack: Hi
Jack: Did you find something to do tonight?
Jack: Ali, you there?
Jack: Napping?
Jack: I'm not leaving you alone until you text me
Jack: Now, I'm officially worried.
Jack: please take a sec to text me an emoji or something
Jack: Now, I am getting pissed. TEXT ME!

I notice two missed calls from Jack, too.

"Who's Jack?" Clay asks. "Were you supposed to do something with him tonight?"

Both sets of eyes are glued on me, waiting to hear my answer. "Let me shoot him a text," I state.

Me: Last minute plans. No pockets. A friend held my phone. Having fun. Sorry
Jack: Cool. Deets tomorrow.

I place my phone beside my fresh mug. Four very intrigued eyes greet mine. "Jack is my little brother. We text every evening or two. Last night, I told him I had no plans tonight. That's why he worried when I didn't respond." I shrug my shoulders.

The relief visibly washes over both guys. *Were they worried as friends, or were they jealous?*

"I think Jack worried the criminals of the big city had attacked me." I try to lighten the mood.

"So, your brother is protective?" Tyson asks.

"Honestly, he never gave me the time of day until I moved here," I share. "When I reached out to him with my new contact information, he began talking to or texting me every day or so, and although he is younger by four years became my protective brother."

The two men share a look—I can only assume is one of relief. Relief that Jack isn't a boyfriend and relief that I have someone looking out for me.

We remain at our table the rest of the night. The occasional female or pair of women approach the guys. I am amazed at the audacity of the females who flirt in front of me. They don't know if I am dating one of them. I witness more than one phone number slip into the guys' pockets. I'd never be that forward. It just isn't me. Call me old-fashioned, but I prefer to get to know a guy before I agree to a date, let alone hook-up with him. I don't like the feelings these women stir in me. I don't fully understand it. *Am I jealous I'm not as forward as these girls?* I worry Tyson or Clay will leave our fun threesome for the rest of the night.

After one such female winks over her shoulder at Clay while she walks away, I fake gag. "Do women approach you like this every time you go out?"

Clay nods with a proud grin, Tyson has the decency to apologize. "I'll need to up my game if I plan to date in the future."

"I've wondered something for a while now," Clay confesses. "Have you dated since you moved?" I shake my head and quickly sip my beer, internally praying our conversation moves in another direction.

"You can't sit at home every night, you're new in town. You should go out, meet people, let go, and have fun," Clay advises.

"I need some more time to focus on me," I state. "I'm not ready to put myself out there for others to let me know what they like and don't like about me."

Tyson slides our conversation to safer topics. We discuss the upcoming Royals games. Clay seems confident they will win four of the next six games. The two place a bet on it with me as the witness. The crowd grows, so we decide to call it a night.

I'm nervous on the ride home, I don't want them to see my apartment. I ask Tyson to drop me off at the same spot they picked me up. They don't question it—I am glad. However, I think they know me well enough now, to understand I am keeping things from them. Tyson even pulls away, even though I know they both want to watch me until I am safely in my apartment.

My earlier statement about not being ready to date returns to the front of my mind. I'm honestly not ready for strangers to judge me, but I could handle Tyson or Clay on a date. The walls I attempt to keep up, quickly fell with these two men. I don't feel as if they judge me. They ask questions in an attempt to get to know me better. They already know me well enough to know when to back off.

They don't know why I am here or why I am hesitant at times, but they like me. They continually chat with me at work and invite me out. I know I should not hope for more with either of my bosses, but despite all of my attempts, I can't stay away like I should.

It seems that the more I try to keep my life uncomplicated, I find myself falling deeper into their web. I continuously find myself drawn to both men. I can't escape their gravity. What's a girl to do?

CHAPTER TEN

Ali:

Thursday evening, my cell phone vibrates on the counter near my simmering soup on the stove.

Jack: Answer the door
Me: What?

I jump at the sound of pounding on my apartment door. Peering through the peephole, I squeal at the sight of my little brother.

"Jack!" I shriek, throwing the door open.

He wraps me in a bear-hug, spinning me around and around.

"What are you doing here?" I crane my neck to look outside for others.

"It's only me." His statement settles my worry that my parents might be with him. "Your secret is still safe—no one knows where you ran off to." He pats my shoulders before taking in my tiny abode. "Wow, Ali, you've outdone yourself. It's lifestyles of the poor and lonely."

His words should hurt, but I'm proud to be on my own, making my way in the world. I can barely afford this place, but I am pleased to still be here and not on my way to Hannibal with my tail between my legs.

"Why didn't you tell me you were coming?" I swat him playfully on the upper arm. Even during my brief touch, I can feel his biceps. My little brother changed in the year I've been away. Not only is he taller, but he filled out a lot.

Jack drops his backpack on my sofa. "It was spur of the moment. The guys were coming to look at colleges, so I told mom and dad I am on college visits. The guys dropped me off, and they'll call to pick me up Saturday afternoon." He pulls a glass from the cabinet and fills it at the tap. "Aren't you happy to see me?" He feigns rejection. I spot the twitch in the corner of his lips.

"I can't tell you how excited I am you'll be here two nights. What would you have done if I wasn't home?"

"Seriously?" He asks. "We text every day or two. I know you hide in this apartment alone more often than you should." He wraps his arm around my shoulders with a squeeze. "I came to rescue you. I'm taking you out and showing you a good time."

I begin to protest, but he insists. "It's mom and dad's money. Let me spoil you. You are working so hard. Let me treat you to a bit of fun."

I love my brother. "What shall we do?"

He suggests I place my soup in the fridge, change out of my pajamas, and we go out to dinner tonight. He'll have me home at a good time as I work tomorrow. Tomorrow night he plans to take me to eat, a movie, and maybe a club if I don't have an adverse reaction from tonight's fun.

The next morning, I sigh as I enter the kitchenette. "I've missed you so much," I confess to Jack as he passes me a doughnut.

"I've missed you, too," Jack returns. "We've all missed you. You should come home for a visit." His eyes pierce into mine. "Or for good."

His words cut. They cut me deep. I can't go back, not yet. I need to heal first. I can't return to that world until I am stronger.

"I'm sorry. Let's change the subject. Your sofa sucks." Jack massages his aching neck, shoulders, and lower back.

I notice pillows and blankets are on the floor. "Jack, I'm so sorry. I should've thought."

"I know money's tight, but that piece of crap must go when you get your first big paycheck." He smiles my way still rubbing his neck. "It's not even comfortable to sit on."

"It just hasn't been a priority. The apartment came furnished, and I had nothing." I explain what he already knows.

"Ali, you don't have to deprive yourself and live this way. Mom and dad will help you. We've talked a lot. They know why you had to start over. If you reach out to them, they'd be here in hours. They love you so much and are very worried about you."

I nod while words clog my throat. I make progress every day but seeing my parents and items from Hannibal would remind me of Leslie. I'm not cured—I'm not ready. Several quiet moments pass.

"Which one?" Jack blurts.

I tilt my head in question.

"Which one are you dating? Tyson? Clay? Or is it both?"

I'd like to think Jack is teasing me, but his expression makes it clear he is genuinely inquiring.

"I'm currently not seeing anyone," I reply grinning.

"But you like them both."

I awkwardly change the subject. "Want to drive me to work so you can use the car today?" Although Jack has no plans, he agrees.

His words haunt me all day. I overanalyze past interactions at the firm. I read into Clay's providing the food truck lunch we share today. I fret about meeting them both for dinner last Saturday. I'm blurring the lines between employee and boss. I so desperately need friends that I don't stay back when I should. I have feelings for both men—feelings an employee should not have for a boss.

Jack plans our entire evening. When he picks me up at the gym at five in an Uber, he informs me we are hitting happy hour on The Plaza, eating barbecue, heading back to the Northland for a movie before finally ending our evening at a bar.

The happy hour scene on The Plaza is not my sort of crowd. However, my conversation with Jack makes it tolerable. He tells me about school, about his friends, about his girlfriend, then mom and dad.

"Crap," I whisper under my breath, my body rigid.

"What?" Jack worries.

"My boss just walked in."

"Which one?" He asks with a chuckle.

"Both," I answer. Just my luck. Jack full out laughs as they spot me and approach.

"Well, well, what do we have here?" Tyson greets.

Clay pats me on the shoulder while giving Jack a nod. I mentally rush through my day to recall if I told either of them my brother is in town. I remember telling Clay but can't remember if I even saw Tyson today as he had court.

"Jack, I'm Clay Ali's temporary boss and this ugly guy is Tyson, her other temporary boss."

"It's nice to meet you. Ali has told us a lot about you," Tyson offers.

Jack tilts his head, his raised brows and cheesy grin scare me. "I've heard a lot about the two of you, also. You should join us." He pushes out an empty chair with his foot as Clay takes the other one.

The guys place drink orders as Jack requests another round for us. I still can't believe my little brother has a fake ID. To make it worse, when we arrived I got carded and he didn't. When our next round comes, Jack is quick to slide his cocktail napkin toward Clay and Tyson. The waitress wrote her cell number and time she'd be off on it. I shake my head at his manly pride.

I sit back watching the conversations between the three guys in my life. I try not to comment on their discussion of hot ladies in our vicinity. I even allow Jack to talk them into joining us for barbecue. Tyson and Clay rave about Jack Stack Bar-B-Cue here on The Plaza.

I grin as Jack and Clay lead the way chatting nonstop. Tyson hangs back beside me. "He makes you smile."

"I've missed him," I confess.

"How long is he in town?"

"He'll leave tomorrow night." I look down at the sidewalk. Our time together is flying by. I don't want him to leave. Tyson nudges my arm with his elbow. No words are spoken. There are no words to make me feel better. Jack has to go back to Hannibal, and I need to stay in KC. I'm not able to visit him, yet. His schedule doesn't permit him to visit me more often. It is what it is.

After dinner, Tyson invites everyone back to his place claiming it much too early to call it a night. Clay asks Jack and me to ride with them. It is then I realize every one of us shouldn't drive. Sensing my hesitation, Clay announces they are using Uber this evening. Jack looks to me with hopeful eyes, so I agree to head to Tyson's.

I've been to Stephen's home to watch his two children—going to Tyson's home to hang out is very different. At Stephen's I worked, if you can call playing with two adorable kids work. I will not be working in any way tonight at Tyson's. I am so caught up in this web I'm now going to my boss' house. Blurred lines become invisible lines.

Tyson's apartment is the penthouse of a new high-rise condominium. That's right. I'm in my boss' home. I am so out of my league here. He gives us a quick tour while Clay fixes drinks. I can't believe the size—my entire studio apartment fits in his living room. I take in the sleek black furniture with its white, gray, and red accents filling the space. It's a bachelor's pad. The newest model electronics are gigantic. Except for a frame on his nightstand of Laila and Joe, there are no pictures to be found in the entire space.

Tyson turns the Royals game on the big screen with the sound very low. Jack and I sit on the black leather sofa while Tyson and Clay occupy the matching chairs. Conversation flows from the Royals to the Cardinals to the Chiefs, then onto other teams in the leagues. Although I follow sports, their discussions are too in depth for me. So, I excuse myself to the restroom.

CHAPTER ELEVEN

Tyson:

In Ali's absence, Jack's liquor loosened lips inform us that when Ali left Hannibal she didn't tell her parents she was leaving or where she was going. They still have no idea. They don't have her new phone number or address. Jack is the only one with her cell phone number.

"I will share more if I have time, but you need to know tomorrow is a very bad anniversary for Ali. I'll need both of you to help me entertain her all day and after I leave tomorrow night. I don't know what to expect as this is the one-year anniversary, but I know she will be very upset," Jack quickly shares while constantly watching the hallway for Ali's return.

"What happened? Why did Ali leave Hannibal?" I ask as she re-enters the room.

"Talking about me?" Ali scans our guilt-filled eyes.

It's clear we are pumping Jack for information. I need to know. I need time alone with Jack. Ali speaks before any of us can think of an excuse.

"I just needed a new start. I debated whether I should go to St.

Louis or Kansas City. I chose KC because it's farther away." Ali's eyes bore into Jack's to keep him from sharing anything further. She points our conversation in another direction.

The night passes quickly. I am unable to speak to Jack privately. Around 1 a.m., I arrange for Uber to take the two of them to Ali's apartment. Ali is exhausted.

CHAPTER TWELVE

Ali:

Jack pulls his head out from under his pillow on my floor late Saturday morning. After a cup of coffee flows into his system, he suggests we head out for brunch. I marvel as he doesn't seem to be paying the price for drinking too much last night. I worry that drinking isn't a rarity for him as it should be for a minor.

As we walk to a diner in the neighborhood, I notice Jack texting on his phone several times. It's probably his girlfriend. He's here two nights, and they can't stand to be apart. Thoughts of my past relationships flood my brain. I miss being in a relationship. I miss the connection with another person that makes it difficult to be apart.

Midway through brunch, Clay happens to walk in. Jack waves him over, and he sits in the booth beside me. I fear it's not the coincidence that Clay plays it off to be.

When the waitress approaches, Clay orders coffee and declines food. I smile as he begins eating bacon from my plate. "Would you like some French toast?" I offer sliding my plate in front of him.

"Only if you aren't going to eat it," he mumbles around his

mouthful of bacon. He doesn't wait for my reply he immediately begins using the fork to cut the bread and stir it in the syrup.

I bite my lip, looking at Jack as I fight the laughter threatening to bubble up. The familiarity Clay displays sharing my meal catches me off guard. It seems intimate. I fear it demonstrates to Jack that my relationship with Clay is much more than I divulged. As Jack stares at me, I shake my head. The corners of his mouth curve upward. Clay consumes every morsel from my plate. I wonder if he'll resort to licking the syrup from the plate next.

"What's next on the agenda?" Clay asks Jack further proving my theory that it is not a coincidence he found us.

"Let's head to the park for a while. We can decide what to do while we're there." Jack replies with a slight grin.

It's a beautiful, sunny, Late-April day. The warmth of the sun caresses my face, arms, and bare legs. I spot an empty park bench near the path. I sit, motion for the guys to join me, and scan the park people watching. In the open area Frisbees fly, others play catch, and couples walk their dogs.

"Someone looks happy." Tyson's voice interrupts my scanning of the scene. He waves at me then executes a chin lift toward Jack and Clay.

"The gang is all here," I announce. I'm on to their scheming.

It's definitely no coincidence—Jack planned this. I suspect he told them what today is. Bile slowly eases up my throat. Heat washes over me from head-to-toe. Tears fill my eyes, but I fight my emotions to prevent their spilling over to my cheeks. I pull in a slow, steady breath as I rise from the bench. Jack calls to me; I wave him off. I need a minute. I need privacy. I place my hands on a nearby oak tree. As I lean toward the bark, I attempt to control my breathing. If I can control my breathing, I won't lose it.

Moments pass, I slowly turn to walk back towards my brother, but a dog sitting near my feet distracts me. I think it resembles a German-Shepard like the one we had when I was in elementary school. I kneel at a safe distance, bow my head, and place one fisted hand between us.

I ignore Tyson yelling at me to move away and Clay trying to coax me closer to them. I can make out Jack's voice, but not hear his words.

I feel the warm dog breath on my fist moments before a hot tongue gives me a tentative lick then pulls away. I slowly raise my head. The dog sits mere inches from my hand. A smile creeps upon my face as I notice the collar and tags on it. It belongs to someone. I can help reunite him with his owner.

With twitching alert ears, the dog tilts its head trying to decipher my movements and intentions. "Come here," I order patting my thigh. I don't have to repeat the command. The gorgeous fawn-colored specimen, with a black mask, approaches. I again fist my hand but hold it close to my chest this time. The dog stops inches from my folded knees and whimpers.

"Good boy...or girl," I chuckle. The dog whimpers again. I slowly open my hand moving it toward the snout. I'm allowed to pet its long nose slowly.

With speed, faster than I can react to, the dog tackles me to the ground and begins licking my cheek then neck. As I giggle, the dog continues lavishing me with love. My brother and friends approach quickly, worried it's an attack by the mighty beast. Once they interpret the situation, they laugh with me.

"I told you." Jack's voice announces. "She's always had a way with dogs."

"Apache, come!" An unfamiliar male voice demands. The sheer volume and timbre of the voice strikes fear in me. "Apache, come."

The dog freezes next to me on the grass. A whimper escapes when it looks from me to the male and back. Strict training prevails. The dog slowly returns to its owner.

"I'm sorry. Is your friend hurt?" The stranger asks the guys.

I dust myself off as I rise from my supine position on the ground. "I am fine. I'm a little wet, but fine," I answer.

Jack and Clay burst out laughing. Tyson mumbles, "Grow up."

I then realize I should choose my words better. "Is Apache a male or female?"

"Male, mam."

Mam? Ouch. My mother is a mam, not me. It dawns on me then that mam and Apache hint to military training. "He's very affectionate, is he a police dog?"

The stranger looks from me to Apache several times. Apache watches his face and whines. "Go."

Apache approaches my side then lifts a paw in greeting. I slowly bend to shake the proffered leg. I sit down, and Apache attempts to sit in my lap. As I laugh, the stranger begins apologizing once again.

"I've never..." He removes his hat, wipes his brow, then replaces it. "He's a military-trained K-9. He's a Malinois and trained to obey at all times. He rarely shows emotions and especially not since we arrived back stateside."

I see the man is baffled. Jack informs him, dogs gravitate to me. Back home I'm known as the dog whisperer.

"I'm Ali," I direct first to Apache then toward the stranger. "This is my brother Jack and my friends, Tyson and Clay." I continue stroking Apache's back and belly while accepting an occasional dog kiss.

The stranger introduces himself as Thomas. Many questions form, but I bite them back. I sense pain in him. I also sense Apache's stress. My mind swims with horrifying images that these two may have experienced.

The four guys chat for a bit, I pay them no mind. Apache allows me to stroke him. I speak of his striking dark eyes, his strong masculine build, and his noble stature. I coo in his ear telling him how gorgeous he is and how I wish I had a dog just like him. We are in our own little world.

"I'm sorry, we have an appointment." Thomas states. "Apache, come."

I immediately miss my furry new friend. Dogs are a source of stress-relief for me. With Apache returned to his owner, the reality of the day floods through my veins again. The bile begins to rise and my hands tremble.

Apache tilts his head and whines at me. He knows. He knows what I feel. The magnificent canine hurts for me.

Thomas begins walking away, commanding Apache to follow. After a slight hesitation Apache obeys.

Jack wraps his arms around me. His hug doesn't soothe me. Today, nothing will. "I want to go to sleep and not wake until tomorrow," I whisper into his chest.

"I know, honey. I know." Jack replies. I stay in his arms for several moments before wiping the tears from my cheeks. "We're going to hang at Tyson's today. Eat junk food, watch movies or baseball, maybe play a game. Nothing overwhelming. We will keep it simple."

I nod, too upset to argue with him. Jack keeps me tucked to his side. I keep my head down to prevent the guys seeing me like this.

In Tyson's SUV, I attempt to regain my composure. My tears stop and my breath evens out. I break the uncomfortable silence by announcing, "I think I should get a dog."

All three guys discuss the pros and cons of my becoming a dog owner. The overall consensus is I would be safer, have company, and be happier so I should look into it. I have a huge problem though; I can't afford a dog. Most weeks I barely afford to eat myself. I decide I'll table the dream of owning a dog until I find a steady job.

At Tyson's, I fling myself on his sofa, grab the remote, and flip through channels for a ballgame to watch. I cringe as sad Lifetime Movies, sappy love stories, or romantic comedies seem to play on every channel. He

has entirely too many channels. I toss the remote before I make my way to the restroom.

Tyson and Clay deliver snacks and drinks to the coffee table as I return. I snuggle close to Jack as we watch the Royals game. The guys keep conversation flowing and tease each other often. I enjoy watching Jack get along with them so easily. Their interactions distract me a little. I lift my head from Jack's shoulder at the ping of the elevator.

"Expecting company?" Clay asks Tyson. "Did you forget you had a booty call?" Through our laughter, the elevator doors slide open.

"Hello," a woman's voice sing-songs into the penthouse.

"Mom?" Tyson cringes.

"Darling," she greets walking further into the space. "Oh, you have guests." She smiles in our direction. "Clay honey is that you?" Her excitement level rises. "It's been too long. You've been too busy with the gym to visit. Come here and hug me." Her arms fly wide as her handbag plummets to the floor.

"Mom, why are you here?" Tyson bites.

As she embraces Clay rocking back and forth, she lets a tinkling laugh escape. "You look good, Clay. Owning the gym is agreeing with you." Turning to her son, she places her hands on her curvy hips. "As for you Tyson, can't a mother drop in to see her son from time to time? You're being rude. I raised you better than this. Introduce us please." Her fingers fly back and forth between her and us.

As he approaches his mother, I press my lips together to keep from giggling. Ironic that this boy hopping up to do as his mother commands is the same lawyer that rudely addressed me my first days on the job.

Tyson places a kiss on his mother's cheek then slides his arm around her shoulders. "Mom, I'd like you to meet Ali and her brother Jack."

Jack and I rise from the sofa to address her. "So, nice to meet you," I state extending my hand to shake hers. "I think we spoke a few times on the phone."

Her face pinches. She looks to Tyson for details. "Mom, Ali is the receptionist covering while Ray is on maternity leave."

"I just dropped our baby gift and held that precious little one for an hour." She beams up at Tyson. "When are you going to gift me with more grandbabies. Joe is six now; I need more little ones."

Clay swats Tyson on the back. "Better get busy, dude," He teases.

"Mom..." Tyson's warning tone is clear.

"Ali from the office. Yes, we have spoken a few times." She ignores her son. "I hope Marshall and my sons are treating you well."

A loud laugh escapes Jack. He remembers my call to vent about Tyson's behavior early in my work there.

"I love it. I will be sad when Ray is ready to return." I don't lie. I had a rough start, but that quickly passed.

"Oh, my goodness!" Tyson's mom proclaims. "You're Laila and Joe's Ali. My grandbabies speak of you often. 'Ali did this.' 'Can you believe Ali played this?' And so on." She extends her arms to me. "Get over here, you."

I cautiously approach, shooting a look Tyson's way. His eyes are as bright as his smile. His mother wraps me in a hug.

"You make my grandbabies so happy. Wait until they hear I met you today. I can hear them now."

"Mom," Tyson attempts to untangle his mother's grasp on me. "Would you like something to drink?"

While Tyson fetches her drink, she joins us on the sofa. I ask her about Ray's baby, and she shares pictures on her cell phone.

"I know," she blurts. "Ali, Jack, Clay, you'll join us for dinner tomorrow at the house." She turns to her son.

"Tyson, you'll see that our guests find their way, won't you?" Before we can object she continues, "Now, I know everyone is busy, but you'll do this to make an old woman happy."

How can we argue with that? She's a force, that's for sure. About five-foot-five-inches tall in her heels—she doesn't take no for an answer. I'm stunned at Tyson's wielding to her suggestions so easily. He's a good son.

Jack informs her he will be heading back to Hannibal tonight. Tyson's mom seems sad at this news. She makes him vow to visit the next time he's in town. She rises from the sofa and orders Tyson to walk her out. With a quick good-bye, she's on her way down in the elevator.

"Time to change the elevator code," Clay hollers to Tyson.

Tyson only shakes his head. I'm sure he is embarrassed she interrupted our afternoon, but she didn't stay long and was a delight to see. It was a welcome distraction.

Jack's phone buzzes several times in his pocket, this is the text I dreaded all day. His friends are close—it's time for him to head home.

"I don't want you to go," I whine pulling him in for a hug.

Jack apologizes and promises to visit again soon. He says his good-byes and thanks to the guys for a great weekend. I walk with him to the elevator, wishing I could fit in his backpack and go everywhere with him.

But, I don't want to go to Hannibal. I'm not ready. Maybe someday I will be strong enough to visit. However, today is not that day.

Jack states he prefers to say good-bye here. He thinks a quick one will be easier for us both. I wrap him in one more hug and promise to keep calling or texting. I don't hide the rivers of tears upon my cheeks. When the

elevator doors close, I feel like my heart sinks with the elevator.

Two muscular arms pull me into a tight hug, tucking the side of my face against his chest. As the tears continue to fall, two more masculine arms join in the embrace. Although I appreciate their gesture, I am too cramped and become hot quickly. I extract myself. Tyson grabs a water bottle from the kitchen while suggesting I stay to watch the end of the game. In no shape to drive through my tears, I agree.

I sit between them on the couch, staring at the giant flat screen not seeing any of the ballgame. My heart hurts as it pounds in my chest. It feels like I left Hannibal again today. Having Jack here made me miss home. I let out a long, deep sigh.

"Wanna talk about it?" Clay offers.

I shake my head unable to speak. I need to leave soon. I need the refuge of my tiny apartment, my comfy PJs, my pillow, and my bed. I want to fast forward to tomorrow.

Tyson places a pint of ice cream in my hand with a spoon. I raise my eyes to meet his questioningly. I didn't know he left my side. I take the ice cream and spoon, sampling a quick bite. Yum. Yes, I need this. I will eat the ice cream then head out to the safety of my apartment.

"It's a bribe," Tyson states. "You get to eat the ice cream, but you have to eat dinner with us tonight."

I don't look up from the pint of chocolate-peanut butter swirl. How did Tyson know this was my favorite? "Jack told you, didn't he?" Tears fill my eyes with the knowledge the guys prepared for this anniversary more than I did.

"Jack didn't give details. He simply stated today would be difficult for you as it was the one-year anniversary of a tragedy," Clay explains. "He texted us some ideas of ways to help you. Your favorite snacks, ice cream, and asked that we keep you company tonight since he couldn't stay."

"He's a good kid and a great little brother," Tyson adds. "We're glad to help and will be here for whatever you need." His large hand plays with my ponytail.

"Can I try a bite of that?" Clay asks.

I spoon a big bite containing peanut butter ribbon in the chocolate and raise it to his lips. No way I'm giving up my spoon or handing over the pint. My phone buzzes in my back pocket.

Jack: I need to confess something, promise not to be mad?
Me: What did you do?
Jack: I left $5000 in your freezer
Me: Why?
Jack: I emptied your account with your debit card before I came. I knew you could use the funds.
Me: That's not my money
Jack: It is. They put it in there while you were at college. They didn't take it back.
Me: I won't use it.
Jack: You NEED a reliable car.
Me: I like Gertrude
Jack: Please set my mind at ease, buy a better car. You live in KC I need to know you are safe.
Me: I am safe
Jack: How many times has Gertrude not started?
Me: a few
Jack: I need a number
Me: fine I will look at a car
Jack: Thank you
Me: I'm mad at you
Jack: Send me pic of new vehicle
Me: If I don't?
Jack: I will tell parents where you are
Me: Ouch. You better not
Jack: They are worried
Me: I'm fine
Jack: They don't know that. Put their fears to rest soon, please

Me: I'm leaving this conversation.
Jack: Sorry. Luv Ya

I find Tyson and Clay watching my closely as I lay my phone on the table and relax into the back of the sofa.

"You feel like talking?" Tyson encourages.

"I need to finish the ice cream first," I whisper.

Tyson nods. Clay informs me there are two more pints of ice cream in the freezer. Wow. They must think I will lose it tonight if it requires three pints of my favorite ice cream. Through my sideways glances, I notice the worry creasing their brows. As hard as it might be, I need to explain. I fear their fears are worse than my real horror.

I place my half-eaten pint in the freezer next to the other two. I grab another bottle of water, then return to the sofa between the guys.

"Do you have a box of tissues?" I ask Tyson. He promptly fetches a new box from the pantry. "Before I begin..." I struggle to pull in a breath. Clay pats my thigh. Tyson scoots closer to my side in support. Here I go. "I don't want to draw out your worry. Before I tell my story, you need to know nothing hurt me physically. I wasn't attacked or anything like that." I look into Clay's deep blue eyes, hoping to see relief.

"Leslie was my neighbor and best friend from middle school to college. We went everywhere together, spent nights at each other's houses, our families even vacationed together. Her parents didn't want her to attend college far away, so we chose the college in Hannibal with the stipulation that we live on campus. We were always roommates and with the same major, took all of our classes together. Looking back now, I realize how unhealthy we were to be together for everything." I pause for a long drink of water. My hands shake so much I can't screw the cap back on. Tyson fixes it for me.

"Last spring, I returned from the library with the books we needed for a paper we were writing. Leslie was to gather snacks for studying while I was out." I exhale a shaky breath. Tyson silently squeezes my shoulders in support. "I unlocked the dorm room prepared to rid myself of the overly heavy backpack." I close my eyes tightly. "I froze in the doorway. There was so much red. Red on the floor, red on the comforter, red on Leslie. I darted to her side. On my knees, I pulled her to me screaming for someone to call 9-1-1. I rocked her back and forth screaming over and over call 9-1-1. Leslie didn't move, her eyes didn't open, and she made no sound. I attempted to wrap her forearms in clothes from the hamper. Everything I touched was red. My hands and arms were red. My jeans were red. Everything sticky and red."

"When the medics arrived, they had to pull me away and sat me on my bed. The resident advisor tried to talk to me while I watched them work on Leslie. I don't know a word she said to me. I heard 'no pulse,' 'too much blood,' 'radio dispatch.'"

"I didn't see the signs. I didn't know she hurt so much. I thought we were living the young, carefree, college life we always dreamed about. My best friend and roommate was in so much pain she felt suicide was her only way out. I failed her."

Clay pulls me onto his lap, wraps arms around me, and rocks me back and forth trying to quiet my sobs. As good as this feels, I need to finish. I need to spill it all, so I can attempt to tuck it far away again.

Through my sobs, I continue. "My parents took me home. Family and friends dropped by to offer condolences, but it just made it worse. My physician prescribed medication to calm me. I know I attended her funeral, but I was so out of it, I remember nothing. My parents arranged incompletes in my classes. I asked Jack to go with me to box up my dorm room. They had cleaned

it, but in my mind, I still saw the thick red blood everywhere."

"Jack was great. He boxed up quickly stating if he grabbed something that wasn't mine, he'd run it next door. I couldn't bear the thought of facing Leslie's parents. He got me home, tucked me in bed with a glass of water, and he unloaded my boxes in the garage." I pause to blow my nose and wipe my tears.

"I slept for hours. I slept way too much. When I woke an envelope with my name on it leaned against my cell phone on my nightstand." I gulp more water. "I recognized the handwriting and Leslie's stationery. Jack had found it while packing my desk. He thought I should read it in private." I climb from Clay's lap, positioning myself between the two men. "Leslie left me her suicide note. Only Jack knows about this. I couldn't bring myself to share it with her parents. I feared they already resented me for not being a better friend."

"Leslie told me she was gay in the ninth grade. She didn't come out to her parents until Christmas break our freshman year of college. She struggled for a few years, then embraced her desires and started dating. Over time she found she was actually a bi-sexual. College allowed her to explore her sexuality more without the constant lies to her parents. She had a guy on the football team she liked, but she never could find the right girl for her. She had several messy break-ups. I learned a lot about how crazy ex-girlfriends can be—she shared the good and the bad with me. I often had to beg her to shut up when she started sharing how hot her sex with a guy or girl was."

I fidget in my seat, pulling the envelope out of my back pocket. I haven't opened it since Jack and I hid it away. I can't bring myself to throw it away. It was Leslie's last thoughts and words. She wrote them for me. I slide it to Tyson and stand. "I need something stronger than water," I state walking away. Clay scoots closer as the

two read Leslie's deepest secret—the reason for her suicide.

I easily find Tyson's liquor cabinet in the dining room. I notice vodka bottles sitting by tumblers on top. I browse the bottles ranging from amber to black liquids in the lower doors. Anyone of them will do the trick. A couple of shots will help to numb my mind a bit on this horrific anniversary.

I nearly jump to the ceiling when Tyson speaks beside me. "Tequila always does the trick." He pulls the bottle out, grabs some shot glasses, then strides to the kitchen. He lines the shot glasses up, pours the liquid, then out comes the salt and fresh cut limes.

Clay slips the folded envelope in my back pocket and plops heavily onto the barstool beside me. "So, let me guess." His words cut into the uncomfortable silence. "She never once let you know she had feelings for you?"

I nod.

"All those years, she kept you so close, but was too afraid to tell you how she felt." He wipes his hands down his face. "That's fucked up."

Humorless laughter escapes me. "Right?" I agree. "I mean we shared everything. She told me details, I never wanted to hear, and she knew it. Even when we drank too much, she never hit on me or expressed her feelings. I've gone over everything from age 13-23 a million times. If her feelings were so strong for me, why didn't she tell me, hint to me, make a pass at me?" I groan. "Growing up we shared beds, dressed in front of each other, and a couple of times when we over-slept we shared a shower—she never once let me know how she felt towards me."

Tyson remains quiet as he slides a shot glass to each of us. In unison, we salt, shoot, then suck our lime wedges. "I mean I don't know how I would have reacted. If she made a move, I know I wouldn't have slapped her or never spoke to her again. If she confessed her feelings,

I'd like to think we would have talked it out for hours with cookie dough and ice cream. I didn't feel that way for her, but I would never have hurt her for being honest with me."

Tyson slides another shot to each of us. Salt. Shot. Lime. This time I feel the burn coat my insides. Now we are getting somewhere.

"Carrying around that note has been a heavy weight on you, hasn't it?" Tyson states more than questions. At my nod, he continues. "I think you should share it with her parents." As I open my mouth to argue, he covers my lips with his fingertips. "Let me explain. They probably question everything they've done as parents wondering what they did to cause her suicide. They need closure. Leslie's final thoughts on paper will give them the answers and the closure they need."

"You wouldn't have to see them or go to Hannibal," Clay offers. "We could mail it to them. You wouldn't even have to write them a note. Her words explain everything."

I fight the urge to scream 'You don't understand! You can't under-stand!'. I play with my empty shot glass admiring the kitchen island lights reflecting in it. It is exhausting keeping this secret, protecting the envelope, and hiding from my former life. Even now the folded envelope feels like a heavy anvil in my pocket. There is never a night I didn't look at the drawer of my dresser knowing it lies inside. It's the last thing I received from Leslie.

Tyson's words jolt me from my thoughts. "Hey, man you home yet?" His dark brown eyes look to me as he listens. "Well, why don't you ask her?" He passes me his cell phone. I note Jack's number on the screen.

"Hi." My weak voice croaks.

"You hangin' in there?" I feel the true meaning of his words.

"Ya, I've eaten half a pint of ice cream, spilled my guts, shared the letter, and downed two tequila shots."

"You've been busy. I wish I could have stayed." Jack confesses.

"I know, but you did the next best thing. You plotted with my two bosses to plan my afternoon and evening."

"I had to do something. I would never have forgiven myself if you were alone in your apartment today. Forgive me?" He pleads.

"There's nothing to forgive." I rise from the stool walking toward the floor to ceiling windows for more privacy. "They want me to mail the letter to her parents for closure." I stand at the window not paying attention to the skyline.

Jack admits it might help me and is something Leslie's parents deserve to see. He tells me to take my time and listen to my heart. If I need to keep the letter, they will understand.

"It hurts to keep it. It haunts me every night, hidden in its drawer. I can't bring myself to destroy it."

"Don't destroy it. If you can't keep it anymore, send it to Leslie's parents," Jack orders.

"We'll see." Gone a couple of hours and I already miss my brother so much. "Thank you for coming to see me."

"No, need to thank me. I missed you, so I came." I know he came more for my benefit than his.

"Thanks for keeping my secrets, too. I know it has to be hard to live with mom and dad with the burden I placed on you."

"Ali," Jack calls to me. "I'm going to hang up, and you are going to watch movies, play games, drink, and relax with the guys. I know it hurts more today, but you need to live. Leslie wants you to live. She wants you happy. She'd want you to focus on the happy memories. You should be sharing happy stories today. The two of you had so many of those. I love you."

"I love you, too."

"Call me if you need me. Otherwise, I'll chat with you tomorrow night." Jack hangs up. I wipe tears from my cheeks before returning the phone to Tyson.

"One more?" Clay asks motioning to the shot glasses. I nod.

I plop back on the barstool. "Jack thinks I should mail the envelope." I let out a huff. "Do you have an envelope I can use?" I look to Tyson. He signals for us to take our shots, then he disappears to his home office.

Clay doesn't speak; he stands behind me placing his hands on my shoulders. Tyson returns setting an envelope with a stamp on it and ink pen in front of me as Clay squeezes my shoulders.

"You have the heart of a fighter. You can do this," Clay whispers in my ear. His hot breath draws goosebumps on my neck.

With pen in hand, I write, 'Mr. And Mrs. Hopkins, 11202 W. Lakeshore Drive, Hannibal MO 63401'. The pen hovers above the return address area. If I put my address, my parents will come for me. If I put my home address...

Tyson chooses to interrupt my inner turmoil. "You don't have to have a return address, but if the post office can't deliver, you don't want it lost as undeliverable. You can put my address or Clay's if you want to remain hidden."

"Jack mentioned your parents understood your need to move away. Maybe it is safe to use your address now," Clay offers.

After several moments, I write my current apartment address in the return area. Clay offers to run it to the mailbox in the lobby for me. I think he worries I might change my mind if it sat on the counter here until tomorrow.

"It feels better," I state. Both men nod. Clay hops in the elevator with the new envelope. I pick up the bottle of tequila, carry it to the sofa, and take a long pull. Tyson

joins me. He removes the bottle from my hands to set it on the coffee table. We enjoy silence until Clay returns.

"Thank you, Clay," I greet. "Thanks to both of you. I dreaded today. Telling you about it helped. I've kept so many secrets this year that I needed to explode." I reach for the bottle, but Clay beats me to it. As I watch him drink from the bottle, I continue. "I feel lighter now. Her parents will receive the letter Monday or Tuesday in the mail. If they see my return address, my parents may be in touch by the end of the week." I sigh as the bottle passes behind my back to Tyson. "I'm not ready to go back to Hannibal, but it felt good to have Jack here. It might be good if my parents came here to visit, too."

Hours later, Tyson suggests we eat before we drink anymore. I watch from the island as Tyson moves deftly around his kitchen warming two take-n-bake pizzas in the oven. Clay places a bag of chips and dip near me along with paper plates and napkins. My tequila-fogged brain enjoys watching these bachelors expertly wait on me. I learn more about each one of them every day.

"I'm tipsy," I giggle.

"We know." Tyson returns setting the timer on the oven. Next, he passes a water bottle to each of us. "Drink up."

"Ali, I've wondered about something for a while now," Clay begins. I tip my head in his direction, squinting my eyes to focus on him better. "Can you explain just how sharing a shower works?"

Tyson slaps him on the back of the head. "Behave." He shakes his head at me. "I apologize on behalf of all mankind."

"Because all mankind would wonder the same thing if they heard me mention it, right?" I tease. "I'm not so drunk that I will add fuel to your perverted fantasies."

"Damn, I thought you WERE that far gone," Clay teases back.

"Are the two of you holding me hostage all night?" I question already sensing the answer.

"I'm offended you aren't pleased with our company," Tyson counters.

"Don't get me wrong, the two of you with Jack's help have done everything right today. It's just I don't have car keys, and I don't have an overnight bag," I inform.

Tyson's eyes widen before he darts down the hall. I look to Clay, but he only shrugs. Moments pass before Tyson returns. "I've placed a change of clothes and fresh towels for you in the master bathroom.

Make yourself at home." He looks to the oven timer then back to me. "Pizzas will be ready in eleven minutes."

I look at myself in the full-length mirror. Tyson's V-neck navy t-shirt hangs loosely. The V dips low on my chest; I'll need to be careful not to bend over. I opt to keep my bra on under his shirt. I swivel from side to side admiring the expensive boxers. I roll the waist once to keep them on. The soft cotton feels good.

My hand quickly rises to my mouth and giggles escape at my thoughts. I now know the answer to the question of whether Tyson is a boxers or briefs guy. In reality, they are cotton boxer briefs, but boxers all the same. My thoughts fly to Clay and his potential underwear preferences. Inquiring minds want to know, but my wandering brain will not learn the answer tonight. I fan my heated face and attempt to gather myself before returning to the guys.

I feel their eyes taking me in from head to toe, even in my slightly inebriated state. "Thanks for the pajamas, Tyson." I grab my water and make myself comfy on the sofa. "Um," I nervously put the lid back on my water bottle. "What are the sleeping arrangements for tonight?"

"Tyson's bed is big enough for the three of us," Clay deadpans.

"It is a huge bed," I recall from my recent wardrobe change. "However, I will not be sleeping with my two bosses," I state matter-of-factly.

Chuckles sound in the kitchen. I am glad they find me funny. I'm dead serious. I might blur the lines, but I won't cross that one. The timer on the oven announces the pizzas are ready. Remote in hand, I flip through the channels for a movie to watch while we eat. Behind me, I hear the sounds of the oven door, a pizza cutter, murmurs as the guys fix our plates, and the sound of a chip bag rustling.

Clay places the chips and dip in front of me, then heads back to the kitchen. The men return with three plates full of steaming hot pizza. One plate sits in front of me along with more water. They're great at waiting on a woman hand and foot.

Much later, I wake to the sound of sirens from the television.

Without moving, I assess the situation. My head lays in Tyson's lap with no pillow. I can see his feet propped on the coffee table. Something heavy presses on my hip. *Is that Clay's head? Are they both asleep?* The room is dark except for the light from the television.

I roll my head around to see Tyson is indeed asleep, his head propped on the back cushion of the sofa. I lift my head a bit, Tyson's hand falls from my hair into his lap. Clay's sleeping head lays on my hip, his arm wraps around my thighs, and his legs extend farther down the couch. He looks much more comfortable than Tyson.

"Hey," Tyson mumbles sleepily. "You okay?"

"Ya, what time is it?" I whisper.

A groan escapes from Clay as he squeezes my thighs tighter in his cuddle. I didn't take tough, boxer, Clay for a cuddly-guy.

"It's late; we should move to the bedrooms," Tyson offers.

I gently brush Clay's blonde locks from his forehead trying to ease him from sleep. He groans again as he swats at my fingers.

"Hey, don't be mean," I chide pulling my hand back out of his reach. "I need to get up, can you unwrap yourself from my body?"

Sleepy-eyed, sexy Clay sits up wiping the drool from the corner of his mouth.

———————

Tucked in the guest bed, I fall asleep to thoughts of cuddly Clay, handsome Tyson, and boxers.

CHAPTER THIRTEEN

Ali:

I need a new place. It's raining cats and dogs, my backseat if full of grocery bags, I must park on the street, walk to the rear of the building then up external stairs to my apartment. At this moment, I hate my life. I might be able to strain to carry all the bags in one trip. I park in the first empty spot at the curb. I'm at the end of the block this adds more steps in the rain.

I scurry from the front seat, close my door, then I open the back door. I duck my head inside as I load my arms. I place four plastic grocery bags safely on my left. I struggle to put the final five on my right arm, pull my head from the dry car, and push the door shut with my full left arm.

Shit! Searing pain radiates from my left temple. I grit my teeth and my eyes water due to the blinding pain. I didn't safely move my head out of the way. The hard metal corner of the door connected with the left side of my face. Leaning against the trunk, I slide myself to the curb before falling. I sit on the concrete curb, rain pelting me, plastic shopping bags still hang over each arm. My world is a blurry view. My heavy head slowly bobbles this way and that. Throbbing pain is all I can focus on at this moment.

My foggy brain knows I need to make my way to the apartment. *Get up!* I slowly attempt to follow the much too loud instructions. *Walk!* I slide my wet feet one in front of the other while balancing the heavy bags. *Climb!* I raise my arms and heavy bags to place my hands on the railing. Each step feels like a trek higher and higher on Mt. Everest. Every muscle in my body protests with each movement. Bongo drums sound inside my skull.

At my door, I drop all shopping bags on the tiny wooden landing to dig out my keys. I slide my purchases into the safety of my space, collapsing nearby. *Call help!* As I lie sprawled out on the floor, I pull my cell phone from my pocket...

"Hmm," I groan squinting at the bright lights.

"Sorry," Clay shoots to the wall flipping off the overhead light.

The dim light of the television illuminates my tiny space. I shift on my bed, moaning at the pain it shoots to my head. "Easy," Clay soothes. He replaces a bag of ice on my forehead. "Lie still," He urges.

I attempt to focus on my surroundings. I'm in my tiny apartment, on my bed, *Clay is here, but why?*

"How..." I whisper. "Why?" I lift my right hand to point at his chest.

Clay shifts his weight on the bed beside my hip. "You've got to lie still and keep ice on your head," he orders in a calm voice. "You called me for help."

Did I? When? Why? I don't remember calling him for help. Crap! I shoot upright. He's in my apartment, my tiny, cheap, nasty apartment.

"Ali, easy. You have to lie down." Clay eases my shoulders to the mattress below me. "You hit your head hard."

Hit my head? Why can't I remember? My head is pounding. I close my eyes, raise my hands to the ice pack, and fight the tears that threaten to fall.

The throbbing at my temple grows. I peek my right eye open. The apartment is dark but the beams of distant street lights. A heavy, hot arm drapes over my waist as a leg twines with mine. I rotate my head toward Clay. My slight movement startles him. His eyes fly open as his hand's dart toward my face.

"Hey," I whisper.

"How do you feel?"

I take a minute to assess the rest of my body. "My head is pounding; my neck feels stiff, otherwise okay." I grin up at his worried brow. "I need to pee."

He carefully assists me in slowly rising to a sitting then standing position. As I trudge to the restroom, his hands never leave my hips. As he pulls the door closed, he warns me to take it easy sitting and getting back up. Silly worrywart.

My heavy head swims and shifts as my world spins. I don't stand. With much difficulty, I pull my shorts up still sitting on the stool. "Clay," I holler as quietly as I can.

My over-protective friend bursts in as if I'm on fire. He escorts me back to bed, forces some over-the-counter pain medication and water down me, then orders me to rest.

"Clay," I whine. "Please tell me what happened."

As Clay places a fresh bag of ice to my left temple, he explains he got a phone call from me at eight p.m. "You slurred your words. I couldn't make out what you were trying to say. You whimpered." He pauses trying to compose himself. "I freaked. I didn't know your address. You met us at the corner when we picked you up weeks ago. I didn't know if you were home or not. I remembered the agency sent me your information in an email, that is how I got here."

He runs his hand over his face. "Your door was standing wide open, grocery bags covered the floor, and you were unconscious beside them. I don't know what happened to you. There were no signs of a break-in, no physical signs of assault, so I removed your wet clothes, tucked you in bed, and iced your head. You don't need stitches; I pressed a cloth to the cut until it stopped bleeding. I've been around my share of facial and head injuries in the boxing world, so I know you'll be okay."

"You have a two-inch cut on your left brow, it's very swollen and a large bruise is forming. Since you don't remember what happened, I suspect you have a concussion. With rest and ice, I'm sure it will all come back to you tomorrow." He gently caresses my right brow

and cheek. The gentleness feels sublime. It gives me something to focus on instead of my pounding headache. "I put your groceries away and mopped up the wet floor."

"Thank you," I whisper.

"Rest," he whispers back placing a soft kiss on my cheek.

Food. I smell food. I struggle to fight the pounding in my head and open my eyes. I squint. My left eye, cheek, and brow feel tight. I first prop up on my elbows taking in the morning light in my apartment. Coffee. I don't smell food; it's coffee. The pain in my head multiplies as I sit up with my feet off the edge of the bed.

"Clay," I lightly call into the kitchen. His head turns, smile upon his face.

"Good morning," he greets. "I have coffee and doughnuts." He offers.

I nod quickly grabbing my head as the pain worsens with movement.

"Take it easy," he orders softly. "I'll bring it to you." He walks my way with hands full of morning delights. "Let's prop you up on pillows." I scoot further back on the bed, resting on the pillows against the wall. "I didn't know what you liked for breakfast, so I settled on a universal favorite." Clay's smile lights the room.

"Thank you," I whisper still holding my head. "Can I take some more ibuprofen?"

He scurries back to the counter. He returns with a bottle of water and three pills in his hand. "I believe the worst is over. You are swollen and bruised, but it doesn't seem to be getting any worse." He tenderly tucks my hair behind my ear, while assessing the area.

"How bruised and swollen are we talking?" I wonder. "Will makeup cover it for work?" I hope I won't look like a freak in public this week. I need the hours.

"Uh," he falters. "The swelling may go down, but the bruising will darken for days before it fades." He tilts

his head hoping his words don't upset me more. I ask Clay to fetch the mirror from my dresser, but he refuses. "Let's wait until afternoon to hold a private viewing."

Crap! How bad must it be if he won't let me look at it yet? I've had bruises before. I know my face is a swollen mess. I need to see it. "Clay, I need to see it. I just hit my head on the corner of the car door. It can't be as bad as you think. I've had bruises before. I can handle it."

He takes another swig from his Styrofoam coffee cup. "So, you remember hitting your head?" He smiles at the return of my memory. I nod and regret it. "Tyson should be here in a bit. When he's here, we will get the mirror."

He called in reinforcements. Crap! Crap! Crap! I place my fingertips on my chin, slowly I allow the tips to walk up the left cheek toward my brow. At the area where my cheekbone should be, I feel soft, swollen flesh and the pain causes me to stop my assessment. My fingertips don't touch my cheekbone, so I'm more than a little swollen. I recall the corner of the door connecting at my temple more than two inches higher. My eyelids feel heavy and swollen, too.

Crap! Now I freak for another reason. It's bad enough Clay is at my place, now Tyson will be here. I've been to Tyson's place; mine doesn't even come close. Any day, I'm embarrassed and ashamed of my living space, today words cannot describe how I feel. I don't want pity. I have issues to work through. I'm making my own way and working on myself. With one call home and my parents would transfer enough money in my account to move almost anywhere. I moan as my tears sting and my head aches.

Tyson doesn't knock but walks right on in. I hope Clay had at least prepared him for my living space. He doesn't stand frozen taking in the area. Instead, he quickly

comes to my side, cringes at my appearance, then pulls me into a gentle hug.

"How do you feel?" He asks hesitantly.

"I hope I look better than I feel, but judging by both your reactions, I fear I don't." I attempt a bit of humor. "Can I have the mirror now?" I ask Clay.

"She wants to look in the mirror. I told her to wait until tonight, so some swelling will go down. She demanded, so I told her when you were here she could look." Clay informs him.

"Ali," Tyson starts.

"Don't Ali me. This is my apartment. If one of you won't go get the damn mirror, I will do it myself." I slide towards the edge of the bed, regretting every movement.

Two sets of arms halt me. Clay goes for the mirror. Tyson situates me on the pillows again.

"A quick look then more ice," Tyson states.

Great. Now two bossy men order me around. I attempt to shoot daggers at Tyson, but fear my injuries prevent the desired menace I hope. Clay's face expresses his unwillingness for me to see myself. I steal the mirror, hold it in front of me, then to my left side. Damn. It's much worse than I predicted. Even if you could take away the swelling, the bruising is atrocious. No amount of concealer and foundation will hide it. I can wear a ball cap, big sunglasses, and my hair toward my face. That might hide most of it. But, I can't work at the firm in a hat and sunglasses. At least at the gym, I can hide in the office. At the firm, I'm front and center. The first person everyone sees. I blow out a huff. The men attempt to console me. I appreciate their words.

"Do you remember how it happened, yet?" Tyson asks patting my thigh.

Before I can reply, Clay responds, "When she woke this morning, she remembered she hit her temple on the corner of the car door."

I attempt to lie down on my bed; the guys help me scoot toward the head of the bed and maneuver my pillows. My every movement hurts. I feel heavy and slow.

"What would you think about hanging at my place today?" Tyson offers. "My sofa might be easier for you to sit or lay on plus Clay and I could sit near you. We could watch movies and just veg for the day."

In other words, my apartment is minuscule, there aren't enough places to sit, and Tyson's TV is ten times the size of mine. Who am I kidding? Even I will be more comfortable at his home.

I nod and regret it. Why can't I remember not to move my head? The guys offer to gather any items I mention. They load Tyson's SUV, then return to assist me.

"I, uh, need to...I'll be right back." I have to use the restroom. Two men hovering make it uncomfortable. I sway a bit as I stand, but four hands hold me in place. I carefully place my hand on furniture and walls as I make my way to the bathroom. They give me my privacy, but I can tell they worry when I am out of sight. I am very dizzy. I return to the kitchen, and they keep hands on me as we walk down the stairs and to the SUV.

I close my eyes on the ride through town. Ibuprofen barely eases the pain in my head. I probably should have gone to the E.R. last night. But Clay's right that I have a concussion—he sees this often in boxers.

I nearly collapse in Tyson's elevator. My dizziness combined with the rising car is too much. Of course, the guys don't let me fall. They all but carry me to Tyson's sofa. I'm propped up with too many pillows, but they are trying so hard I don't complain.

When they join me on the sofa, I ask Clay, "How do you do it? I can't imagine repeatedly dealing with the concussions, the pain, and vertigo. It sucks. And boxers get this all the time."

Clay shakes his head. "First of all, I remind you I don't compete. I work out at the gym. Injuries are infrequent. Secondly, boxing is a sport like any other. Boxers train in an attempt to be the best, win money, and so on. Football players are aware of potential risks and injuries, so are Nascar drivers."

"Whatever, I don't like it. I think guys are nuts if they do anything that might cause this pain."

Tyson weighs in. "Women box, women have semi-pro football teams. It's not just men."

I wave him off. I'm sorry I brought it up. "When can I take more ibuprofen?" I look to Clay.

"Not for two more hours, but you can take some acetaminophen now. We can stagger the two to help manage the pain." Tyson retrieves the two pills and a bottle of water. I down the pills like a good little patient. I pretend to watch the movie on TV, but soon fall asleep.

CHAPTER FOURTEEN

Ali:

I'm more nervous today than I was the first Monday I worked at the firm. Marcia came over last night to brainstorm ideas to minimize my bruises. Makeup won't work, it draws more attention to my face. A hat and sunglasses will bring too many questions. We decided it is best to inform the staff and for me to sit sideways at the desk to hide the side of my face from any visitors.

Tyson took it upon himself to email all staff last night with all the details of my accident in hopes of preventing concerned questions all day. He read the email to me before sending it. His last paragraph encouraged the staff to minimize interactions with me because although I appreciate their concerns, I am self-conscious of the bruises.

Ever blurring the line between boss and employee, Tyson texts me to let me know he is waiting downstairs to drive me to work this morning. While I appreciate their friendship, my feelings for Tyson and Clay are growing more confusing by the day. I fear because of my months of seclusion; I now am over-anxious to be in a relationship. I cherish their friendship and wish I could leave it at that. My body seems to be hyper-alert when they are nearby. I *should* focus on being friends and not blur the lines any further.

CHAPTER FIFTEEN

Tyson:

"I can't tell you how much I like seeing Ali in her office," Clay states before launching a right uppercut.

"I tell her things, I shouldn't share," I confess between jabs.

Clay steps back, places his gloves on his hips, then queries. "Things you haven't told me?" He attempts to look distraught.

"No, you know everything about me. You've always been the only one, until Ali."

"Let's call it good," Clay offers as he climbs through the ropes. "We can hit the showers and get out of here."

We shower, say our good-byes to Ali, then walk to Rock and Run. It's another bright, warm May day. We opt for a high-top table on the patio, order beers, then return to the previous topic.

"Ali is easy to talk to," Clay concurs. "She's unlike any woman I've ever met." He fiddles with his beer mug avoiding my eyes.

"It seems we have a problem," I mumble. "I hoped it would work itself out."

Clay understands my meaning without asking for details. This hasn't happened to us before. We hung in the same circles in high school and college but have very different interests in women. "I've tried to avoid the subject. I think I thought she would give a sign that we might know her desire for one of us." Clay lifts his eyes to mine.

"What should we do?" I implore.

Clay signals the waitress and orders four shots and another round of beers. "Well, I guess we need to see where we each stand and decide from there."

I snicker. "You mean talk about our feelings like girls do?"

We laugh at our predicament. When the shots arrive, we quickly down the first round with a beer chaser. Clay spins his empty shot glass several times like a child's top.

"Ray returns this week, so she won't be at the firm in the mornings anymore," my low voice breaks into the silence. "I'll only see her afternoons I work out at the gym, or if I ..." I don't want to finish. Letting Clay know how much I want to date her might ruin everything.

"I think I can make this easy on us both," Clay announces before downing his second shot. I follow with mine. Clay sees the hope on my face. "I can't lose her at the gym. I'm horrible at paperwork and sitting at a desk. How I ever thought I could be a lawyer, I don't know. Maybe it was a blessing when grandpa passed, and I left law school." He sighs. "I've been thinking about hiring Ali full-time. Not only is she everything I need in an office supervisor, but she has the most creative ideas. I think I can turn the gym around, even turn it black with her on board."

I listen attentively to my friend still wondering how this might ease the growing tensions between us due to our shared interest in Ali.

"If she works full-time at the gym, I don't think I should pursue a relationship with her outside the gym. Don't get me wrong; I want nothing more than to act upon my feelings. I've been struggling with the decision of dating her versus making her my partner at the gym."

I sit straight up. "Partner not just an employee?"

"Ya, she has turned so many things around in the six weeks she's been working afternoons, I'd like to reward her." Clay runs his hand through his shaggy blonde hair. "You've seen her place and her car. She needs a permanent job as much as I need someone to straighten me out at the gym. As a partner, it wouldn't be much now, but soon it could be with her help."

"Dude, I hope you know I'm not a selfish bastard when I say that is a great idea. She does need a permanent job. She loves working at the gym, and I think she might be able to keep your shit in line. I could help you with the legal aspect of the partnership. Did your parents give you sole proprietorship of the gym?" Clay nods. I hope my enthusiasm proves to Clay, it's for the gym and not for his stepping aside where Ali is involved.

"What ideas did she have for the gym?" I'm intrigued.

"She wants to offer a 6 a.m. and 6 p.m. kickboxing exercise class to members and the public. She suggested I start kids boxing league on the weekends. And most importantly, she said I need to remodel to add a women's locker room. Apparently, I am missing out on an entire gender dynamic by targeting men only," Clay replies.

"Wow." I'm not surprised she is more than just a temp. She was seeking a degree in business before moving to Kansas City. "What do you think of all that?"

"I'd be stupid not to follow through," Clay scoffs. "Since I need Ali at the gym, I won't pursue her romantically." He looks to me to ensure I understand he's serious. "With me out of the way, you can make your move."

"Are you sure?" I ask. "Shouldn't we wait to see if she is interested in your partnership first?" If Ali refuses the job, then Clay might want a chance with her. I don't want to act too fast and lose Clay later.

"She'll take it. We both know that. But, if you need more time to get your shit together, you can wait," Clay teases.

"I need to order food." I quickly change the subject. "Should we invite Ali here for dinner and drinks when she leaves the gym?"

Clay picks up his phone, punches a few buttons, then waits for an answer. "Hi, everything going okay at the gym?" He waits for a reply I can't hear but can predict. "Tyson and I walked to Rock and Run wanna join us?" Unaware that his words slur ever so slightly, he smiles across the table. "Great. See you soon." He disconnects. "Your future girlfriend will be here in a few minutes."

"Don't start that shit," I order. "What's to say she will even consider seeing me?"

"Dude why are you always so hard on yourself." Clay knows me. "Baby steps, you'll see it will work out. You should invite her to the gala next weekend."

CHAPTER SIXTEEN

Ali:

When I arrive, the guys are well into their fourth beer and can't recall how many shots they've enjoyed. I order an iced tea when they request their appetizers and entrees.

"Hungry?" I tease. I note the empties on the table as the waitress sends a busboy over to clear them. It seems the guys are out to have fun. "So, what's up?" Clay and Tyson stare at each other for an answer. "Guys," I prompt. "Are we celebrating? Are we getting over a girl? Why are you drinking so much?"

"Um," Clay stutters. "This is your last week at the firm, so we thought we'd treat you to a night of fun."

"You two make me smile," I note. "And I need more smiles in my life." *Where did that come from?* They will think I'm a loon. I can't even play it off as alcohol talking. I scramble to cover for my awkwardness. "I wonder what the agency will have for me next." I think aloud while I try to hide my fear of not being able to pay my bills in a month or two.

As the food and more drinks arrive, we enjoy casual conversations.

After a couple more drinks, Clay states we are going to play 'I've Never.' He announces I go first.

"I've never used Tinder" I begin.

Tyson and Clay both burst out laughing before they drink. I'm not sure what is so funny. Perhaps there's a funny story of a Tinder hook-up. "Well?" I prompt.

"I don't use Tinder, nor have I ever used Tinder." Clay attempts to keep a straight face.

"I don't believe you." I challenge. "Why do the two of you think this is so funny?" I look from Tyson to Clay.

"A while back, the two of us while hanging at my place, signed up for Tinder. We took turns looking at each woman, discussing her, and swiping left or right," Tyson explains. "After thirty minutes we realized we both had only swiped left and never swiped right. We quickly deleted the accounts." He chuckles. "The next night we went out to a couple of clubs. We were approached three different times by women who claimed they saw us on Tinder the night before, swiped right on one of our profiles, and when they looked today to see if they had a match they found we were no longer on Tinder."

"We did it together as a joke. We just wanted to check it out and see how lame it might be. We found some very forward and explicit profiles with only a few normal ones," Clay adds.

"We never planned to use the app as a means to meet women," Tyson testifies. "Neither of us is the type to look for a one-night stand. I think that is why we have lasted as friends so long. We both respect women, the dating process, and realize our ultimate goal is to find a soulmate, not to rack up the most one-night stands."

"Wow. Don't get me wrong. I'm glad the two of you feel the way you do, but I was looking for a yes or no answer," I tease. This may be a fun evening if the alcohol has loosened their lips. I may get answers to many of my questions.

"How about you?" Clay asks throwing my question back at me.

"I never even entertained the thought of using Tinder. It's too easy to mislead others on social media." I think this game would be more fun if I were drinking, too. The guys have consumed enough, that I know I need to be the designated driver tonight. I tell Clay it's his turn.

"I've never had a dating nightmare," Clay offers.

I jump right in. "One summer, my parents went on a two-week cruise of the Mediterranean with Leslie's parents." I'm amazed I shared that fact. I haven't openly talked about Leslie or her family in a year. I take a quick inventory of my feelings as I sip my tea. Seems I'm okay with talking about them now, so I continue. "We stayed on my grandparent's farm a few miles from Hannibal. A friend of a friend asked me on a movie date. I accepted, and he agreed to pick me up at the farm." I shake my head at the memory. "It had been a rainy week. The dirt roads were a muddy mess. He showed up in his father's white sedan. It was a filthy mess when he pulled into the driveway. We were almost late for the movie because he washed the car the moment we hit town. It took everything in me not to blurt out he was an idiot to wash it, as he had to take me back home."

The guys chuckle thinking that is the entire story. "Wait, it gets worse," I promise. "It started raining while we were in the theater. It was still raining as he drove me home. I suggested he drive in the center of the gravel road as that was more packed down than the edges. The city boy in him still drove on the right half of the road. We ended up in a rut that pulled us into the ditch. He attempted to drive in reverse and forward with no luck. As he was wearing a pale pink button-down with white golf shorts and white Sperry's; I offered to walk the mile to the farm to get help. I drove the tractor back, hooked the chain under the bumper of the car, and proceeded to pull him out of the ditch." I make a disgusted face. "The jerk didn't even follow me back to the farm. There was never a second date."

The game continues with the guys spilling secrets about each other as they drink way more than they should.

I purposely didn't drink alcohol and end up using Tyson's SUV to drop the guys off before I take a cab back to my car. I rationalize the expense as okay because they paid for my dinner tonight.

CHAPTER SEVENTEEN

Ali:

Later the next week, Clay pops his head into my office. "Got a minute?"

"I've always got a minute for you, boss," I tease. His reaction to my words makes me think this is not the type of conversation we usually share.

"What's up?" I ask tilting my head to the side a smile on my face.

Clay closes the office door. Fear floods my entire body. I can feel my heart pounding violently in my chest. "I want to ask you a favor," he begins clearing his throat. "Well, it's a favor for me, but you won't think of it that way." His nervousness is very apparent. His arms fold across his chest as his fingers strum on his biceps. "Would you consider working at the gym full-time?" Instantly, he looks more relaxed having spoken the words.

Full-time? He's offering me a full-time job. No more working at the temp agency, no more worrying where my next paycheck might come from or if it would cover my monthly expenses. "Of course," I answer quickly. No need to act nonchalant. He knows I need a job—he's seen my car and my apartment.

"Well, I have another question then." He smiles. "Would you consider coming on as my partner?"

"What would that mean exactly?"

"The two of us would be equal owners of the gym. I can't make it work on my own. You know that. I need a business partner to handle the paperwork, the bills, and keep me organized. We'd be 50/50 partners in decisions and profits." Clay looks like an expectant child asking permission from his parents to go to a friend's house.

"Clay, I don't have the means to buy in..."

"Stop," he orders. "I didn't buy the gym. It was willed to me by my grandfather. I wouldn't expect you to buy into it. Tyson said he would help us with the paperwork." He runs his hand through his unruly locks. I want to be the one to run my fingers through his hair. It seems so soft. "We'd keep doing what we are doing now. We work well together. We plan well together. Your ideas have started to turn a profit. Give us a few more weeks, and we will be rolling in the dough," he chuckles.

Of course, working in the office, I know the balance in his business accounts. I know the current increases in monthly income. I see the potential. It will be steady money for now with the potential to increase in the future. "I'm in!" I shout as I throw myself into Clay's arms.

He wastes no time wrapping me in his arms and twirling us around. A deep belly laugh escapes his mouth. I feel the vibrations rise from his chest pressed to mine. As he sits me down, I wipe the tears of joy from my cheeks. I genuinely enjoy my time at the gym with Clay. The members are great, and there is lots of room for improvements.

I choose this moment to share a secret. "I have a confession," I begin. "I have a notebook at home full of ideas for the gym." Clay's smile grows to reach his blue eyes.

"I can't wait to see it, partner," he promises, excitement twinkles in his eyes.

I can't wait to share the signage changes, removing the black from the windows and door, and much more. I wiggle in my seat at the thought of sharing my ideas with Clay. Partners. He wants me as his partner. We will rock this. Our gym will be the best. With the two of us at the helm, how could it not be?

As I lie in bed, my thoughts run away with visions of Clay and me at work at the gym. I envision the changes to the building and signs, the new classes and leagues, offering our members more, and our future success. Clay and I complement each other well in the work environment. The casual work setting is fantastic. I need to tell Jack.

Me: You still up?
Jack: Ya what's up
Me: Can I call you?

I watch with rapt attention waiting for his reply. I nearly jump out of my skin as my phone rings. I greet my brother and immediately share the details of my talk with Clay about the partnership. Jack seems as excited as I am with the prospect. I share my ideas for the gym—he likes those, too. Then he bursts my bubble of happiness.

"Ali, this means you can't date Clay," Jack states. "As partners, it could ruin the business if it didn't work out."

I agree, and our conversation continues for fifteen minutes more. I place my cell phone on its charger by the bed. I sink into my quilt and the pillows. I'd shared my feelings toward my two bosses often with Jack in the absence of me having other friends. He kept encouraging me to make a move, and I explained I couldn't date my bosses. Crap! *Why hadn't I thought of that?* There is chemistry between Clay and me, I can't deny it. Clay and I will be partners; I can't blur the lines. We can be friends and partners at the gym. I love hanging with him; I love talking with him, I love working with him. I will squash my lustful thoughts starting immediately.

CHAPTER EIGHTEEN

Ali:

I exit the elevator strolling toward the reception desk. *How should I act on my last day at Lennox Law Firm?* If I'm too chipper, they might think I am excited to be done here. If I act down, everyone will pity me. I vow just to be me. I tuck my purse in the empty file drawer then turn the phone off night mode.

Small groups arrive, greet me like any other day, and head into the back office. Stephen pounds his palm on the desk, pulling my attention from the call I just transferred.

"It's not final yet," he starts. "Would you be available tomorrow night if we need a sitter?"

Of, course I'm available. Although my social life sparked to life thanks to Tyson and Clay, I have no plans this weekend. "Yep. Just give me a call or text to let me know details if you need me," I reply. An evening with Laila and Joe is always better than the loneliness in my tiny apartment.

Stephen disappears to the back. One of the legal assistants brings me an iced cappuccino for my last day. Otherwise, the morning's greetings are all normal. I glance at the online schedule—it seems Tyson, Stephen, and Marshall will be in court today. That usually means fewer phone calls and visitors to keep me occupied but, I have my Kindle App for the slow times. Tyson is slated to be in court this morning. I hope he might be in after lunch—it's my last day after all. I want to see him.

My first hour passes at a snail's pace with few calls and no visitors. Instead of reading, I doodle on my notepad. I look up excitedly at the ping of the elevator. A smiling Tyson exits followed by his mother.

"Good morning," I greet unable to hide my wide smile. "The schedule stated you were in court this morning."

Tyson's impish smirk alerts me he's up to something. His mother removes an envelope from his hands and places in on the counter in front of me.

"What's this?" I ask before I turn the sealed beige envelope over. I find my name printed on the other side. I look to Tyson then his mother for guidance.

"It's a gift for you, dear," she prompts. "You've been a blessing to the firm in Ray's absence. We wanted something special to thank you for your time here." She pushes it towards me. Tyson nods.

With a shaky hand, I clasp the envelope; I use the letter opener from my desk to rip at the crease and withdraw its contents. I have to read it twice to comprehend the gift. It seems I will be treated to a spa day, tomorrow from ten to four with a full menu prepaid. I've heard of The Elms Spa—it's supposed to be a haunted hotel. My skin tingles with excitement.

Tyson's mother places her hand over mine on the counter. "Marcia will meet you there at ten. The two of you will relax and pamper yourselves all day."

"Marcia goes there all the time," Tyson adds. "Mom's joined her a few times. You will love it."

Looking into his eyes, I sense his hesitation at my reaction to the gift. I need to put his mind at ease. "You shouldn't have. I only did my job. I received a paycheck, so a gift isn't necessary."

The two explain in the past temps caused more issues than they helped. Some were unreliable, while others refused to work. They believe I went above and beyond at my job.

"Thank you," my voice shakes. I will miss this job and this family. "It is a lovely gift. I haven't been to a spa in over a year. I'm sure I will love it."

While his mother excuses herself to the back office, Tyson remains across the reception counter from me. He rests his forearms on the countertop leaning towards me. He speaks in a hushed whisper. "You deserve a day of pampering. Promise me you'll take advantage of all the treatments Marcia planned for you."

"Um," I nervously clear my throat then I nod.

"I wondered if you might join Clay and me to watch the Royals at my place on Sunday?" His long fingers toy with the pens standing in my pencil holder.

"I would love to," I admit.

"I'll text you tomorrow night with details," he promises.

Just like that my fears of losing Tyson's friendship evaporate. *I wonder if he feared I would vanish into the vast city if he didn't plan an event to ensure we will see each other? Does he worry as much as I do?*

"You wanna give me your number or should I ask Clay for it?" In his voice, I hear teasing along with a bit of jealousy that I haven't shared it with both of them.

I write my digits on a sticky note then slip it into his folded hands. The corners of his mouth turn up instantly. He flashes his dimples my way with his killer smile. I love the way the creases at the outer corner of his caramel brown eyes crinkle. They aren't age wrinkles. They're sexy. Distinguished.

"So, you don't have court this morning?" I ask. "I worried I might not see you before I left today," I confess before I catch myself.

"I wanted you to think I was busy," he states smirking. "Grab your purse," he orders.

Tilting my head slightly I squint at him, "Why do you need my purse?"

"I don't need your purse," he chuckles. "Actually, you don't need it either." He takes my hand pulling me from behind the desk. "My mother and the staff are treating you to lunch. I offered to man the phones."

"Man the phones-good one." I shake my head. "Why treat me to lunch and a spa day? It's too much."

Tyson explains as he holds the glass door open to the back office. "The spa day is a gift from my family. The lunch is a gift from the firm."

I don't know what to say. I can't say a word. Immediately each office staff member begins telling me how they enjoyed my time here, how they will put in a good word for me if I need a reference, and how they will miss me. It takes several minutes for everyone to set the phones to out of office and grab their purses. On our way to the elevator, Tyson tells us to enjoy our lunch, from behind the reception desk. I pause turning to face him with my hands on my hips.

"Do you even know how to run the switchboard?"

"Nope, but I know how to set it to night mode. I am here to greet any visitors we might have." Lifting his hand, he points to the elevators. "Don't you worry. Go have fun."

CHAPTER NINETEEN

Ali:

I arrive at The Elms at 9:50. I slip into the first open parking slot I find. Exiting the car, I walk through the lot searching for Marcia. She waves and hops from her SUV.

"Are you ready for the most relaxing day of your life?" Her cheerful voice greets. She tucks her arm through mine and walks us into the spa. "You will think you have died and gone to heaven. The staff here are fabulous, the food spectacular, and the treatments do everything they promise."

"I used to go to a small spa back in Hannibal with my mother and friends a couple of times a year. I am sure it will pale in comparison. I look forward to relaxing." I want her to know I'm not a spa-virgin.

Entering the reception area, I bite my tongue to ensure my mouth doesn't hang open. The interior feels as if we stepped into a Greek villa. Fountains with trickling water grace the walls in each room. The white walls look weathered by many years on the Mediterranean. Clay pots and vases sit atop pedestals. Faux arched windows seem to contain views of the outer landscape. Painted green vines run from room to room. The reception staff wears Greek-inspired peplos with flat sandals laced above the ankle. They greet us by name at reception, escort us to the locker room, and prompt us to enter the lounge once we change.

We remove our clothes, tie our robes, and secure our items in our lockers. Marcia leads the way to the communal lounge. Upon entering, they offer a choice of a variety of flavored waters. Marcia chooses a chaise lounge—I pick one nearby. Our menus appear. Each explains the order of our services for the day and the name of the staff member providing the treatment.

"Tyson was hilarious planning for this," Marcia states fanning herself with the tri-fold spa menu. "I pulled up the website and ask him to list the items he wanted to

include. His eyes nearly popped out of his head a few times when I explained in detail some of the treatments." She sips her cucumber water before continuing. "Eventually he gave up telling me to sign me up for all of the items I thought you'd want. Now, I don't know you very well, but I chose the deluxe menu. We will have everything you see on yours. Some are optional; you can elect to remain in the lounge or partake as you choose. Just know, Tyson already paid for everything today. So, relax and enjoy it all." She sweeps her arms wide in the room.

"I hope he paid for you to join me today."

"Of course, I am part of your spa package," Marcia laughs. "I told him you might feel more comfortable with a friend joining you. He thought this being my spa; you might like having an expert with you," she explains.

"I am thrilled you joined me today," I state. "It's more fun when we can giggle and gossip, right?"

Before lunch, we enjoy facials, wraps, and massages. Our meal finds us on the private patio with an entire bottle of wine that the two of us empty. During the afternoon, we are buffed, waxed from head-to-toe, then enjoy manicures and pedicures.

Throughout the day, I realize how much I miss my parents' money allowing me to enjoy such perks. Leslie and I treated ourselves to mani-pedis often. Spa days with our mothers happened a few times each year. We usually went around everyone's birthdays and before the holidays. Of course, our mothers treated us to the spa the weekend before our high school prom.

I find my time with Marcia quite pleasant. We speak as if we're long-time friends. She shares the story of meeting Stephen and his family, several stories of Tyson's pranks, and the birth of her two children. I share humorous stories from college parties and my many temp jobs. Luckily, she doesn't pry into my reason for moving to

KC or about my family. She seems content with anything I decide to divulge.

As we wrap up our treatments and change into our street clothes, Marcia informs me Tyson arranged for a car service to pick us up. Next, we're heading to shop. I try to argue but find Marcia a tough nut to crack. She's only following Tyson's directions for the day.

Our driver escorts us to a section of the city I haven't visited. The store isn't one I would ever enter. Marcia speaks in private to a sales lady. We follow our escort to a private lounge and fitting room. As we sit and enjoy a glass of complimentary champagne, dresses are gathered for me to try on. They don't ask my size or preferences—they merely disappear onto the sales floor.

Two metal racks full of dresses make their way back to us. My jaw drops to the floor. Marcia laughs at me as she lifts my chin. She tells me Tyson wants me to choose a cocktail dress with all the necessary items to go with it. She crosses her heart she doesn't know what he has planned for such a dress. I vow to let her help me select one so Tyson won't be upset with her.

I need to have a conversation with Tyson. I don't like surprises. I don't like being forced into things. I like to have an opinion and choice. I don't need his flashy money—it's not the reason I like being near him.

In the dressing room, I try on dress after dress. Red, deep violet, royal blue, Kelly green, emerald green, silver, gold, and many other colors slide on then slip off. Some are short; others are long. I twirl in front of mirrors, sales ladies, and Marcia in strapless, off the shoulder, empire waist, and spaghetti straps. Some sparkle with sequins while others flow with ruffles. It's prom dress shopping on steroids. In the ump-teenth dress, I collapse in the chair next to Marcia with a groan. She passes me a champagne flute. We direct our sales lady as she sorts the dresses onto two racks. The rack of dresses we prefer remains while the other leaves the lounge. A fruit and

cheese platter arrives to give us strength in our selection endeavor.

"I need a few minutes to clear my brain," I state. "I've got too many dresses up here." I swirl my fingers around my head.

Marcia does her best to chat about all things non-dress related while we nibble and sip. The staff arranges our remaining choices on hooks around the room. We've narrowed it down to four. I scan from one to the other remembering how the fabric or style felt and moved.

"Which are your two favorites?" I ask Marcia.

After she answers, I share my two favorites were the same as hers. The personal shopper agrees those looked the best with my height and coloring. I wonder had I chose a different one if her comment would have been the same. She probably agrees with the customer instead of sharing her true opinions.

"I'm drawn to the blue one," I inform Marcia. Marcia hops from her chair clapping excitedly. "I'll take that as a yes on the blue one." I laugh.

While Marcia excuses herself to the restroom, I'm encouraged to try the entire ensemble on one more time in case alterations might need to be made. In the changing room, I pull on the dress, slip on the shoes, and grab the clutch. In the mirror, I turn from side to side. I smile pleased with my choice—if only I knew why I needed a dress.

"Okay, here I come for the last time," I announce while opening the changing room door. Marcia has not returned. The personal shopper isn't present. Instead Tyson leans against the wall in a stunning black tux. My breath catches at the magnificent sight. He styled his dark hair as he wears it to work each day. His dress shirt is royal blue with French cuffs barely visible on his crossed arms. His tie is a complimenting swirl of gold, purple, and blue. As his eyes slide over me, I feel heat in their wake.

"Well," I slice the silence. "How did I do?" I slowly spin myself in a circle so that he might enjoy the entire package. I've never worried so much about my appearance. I don't have enough details to know if I chose a dress appropriate for the event he has planned. I don't know what he prefers.

Without a word, he approaches. He extends his arms taking ahold of mine. He spins me away from him. Pressing tight against my back he whispers into my ear, "Blue is my favorite color. This dress, those heels, I..." I feel his breath upon my neck. My skin prickles. "You look magnificent." I attempt to face him but am prevented by his hands at my waist.

"It's incomplete though." He states.

I look at myself in the nearby mirrors trying to notice what he sees missing. Our eyes lock in the mirror. He slides his hands into his trouser pockets pulling a velvet box from each. Extending his hands in front of me, I look from the mirror to the gifts.

"Your neck and ears are naked," his husky whispers send tingles throughout my body, while heat builds in my core. "I thought you might like these."

I open the earrings and the matching necklace a gasp escaping. With trembling fingers, I place the teardrop diamonds in each ear. Tyson takes the gold chain from my hands and secures the necklace for me. His hot fingertips glide along the chain to the teardrop diamond just below the hollow of my neck.

"Perfect." His words prompt my eyes to lock on his in the mirror.

"You have some explaining to do," I inform crossing my arms and thinning my lips. I turn to face Tyson. "This is too much. I can't accept the jewelry or the dress." I need to nip this in the butt. He is out of control.

Standing so close our toes nearly touch, his eyes scan me one more time. He shakes his head without speaking a word.

"Tyson," I urge. "What is this all about?" I point between the two of us dressed to the nines.

Clutching my hand, he leads me from the private lounge promising answers in the car. The driver opens the backdoor and Tyson holds my hand as I climb into a black sedan. He slides beside me and soon we're off—I still don't know where.

"I must attend a charity event tonight, and I would like for you to accompany me," he states.

I note he didn't ask me ahead of time if I was free tonight. He didn't mention a fundraiser or ask if I might like to join him. He didn't ask me on a date. No, he gifts me a day of pampering and forces me to shop not knowing he planned a night out.

"Is this a date?" I demand from him.

His head jerks to look at me. "I, uh..."

"Tyson, is this how you ask all your women to attend functions with you?" I continue my barrage.

He stammers some more not sure how to respond to my implied anger. I enjoy the look of turmoil on his face. This sure-of-himself bachelor suddenly seems unsure of his actions.

"Cat got your tongue?"

"Ali, I'm sorry. I wanted to surprise you. I thought you might enjoy a night out. I mean with me. Um..." Tyson's voice falters.

"I'm just pulling your chain," I admit. "What function are you whisking me off to this evening?" I notice our driver smiling approvingly in the rear-view mirror at my teasing.

"We are attending the JDRF Gala this evening. It is one of my favorite charity events each year." He confesses. "JDRF is..."

I interrupt his explanation. "Juvenile Diabetes Research Foundation." His soft smile assures me he is impressed with my knowledge. "My friend was a Type-I diabetic. I learned everything I could about it."

"Well, each year the Kansas City Chapter holds a gala with a silent and live auction to help raise funds for the cause. The firm donates once a year, and I offer to attend the gala." He shrugs. "We will enjoy drinks, mingle, dine, and the entertainment will be the extravagant bidding in the live auction portion of the evening," he explains.

"So, is this a date?" I ask barely above a whisper.

"If I hoped this could be our first date, would that be okay with you?" He asks back.

"For future reference, I would prefer you ask me in advance and explain in some detail any event we might be attending. Other than that, I guess we can call this a first date," I respond.

Tyson shakes his head at me smiling. He places his hand in mine on my thigh, and we ride in silence into downtown Kansas City. I enjoy the beauty of the skyline with the setting sun. Our gala is at a hotel. A valet opens Tyson's door and welcomes us. As we enter the hotel, our driver disappears, and Tyson tucks my arm around the crook of his elbow. I love the tingle I feel at his gesture.

Inside, Tyson registers his cell phone and credit card to cover any bids he will place. He hands me a catalog of all silent and live auction items, then putting his hand on the small of my back guides us to the open bar. While in line, Tyson asks if I want a drink. He orders my amaretto sour and his rum and cola. He tips the bartender and escorts me to a high table.

For the next hour, we sift through the displays of silent auction items. Tyson demonstrates how to bid for an item using his phone. I'm surprised when he asks me to hit the bid now button for him. He then shows me how he will place a maximum bid amount on that item. The app will bid for him if he is no longer the highest bidder.

"You have big plans for that dog gift basket you just bid on?" I ask.

"Maybe I will get a dog if I win it," he teases. "I can gift it to someone or hand it to Laila and watch Stephen have a coronary. He claims they will never own a dog. The kids want one, and I keep teasing that I will buy them one."

I can't believe I'm at a formal gala with Tyson. I pinch every penny, and he bids well over the suggested retail price on a pet basket when he doesn't own a pet. We are living in two very different worlds.

From time to time, I pause to look at items of interest to me. A few catch my eye, one is a large basket filled with a new Kindle, bottles of wine, bubble bath, scented candles, a fluffy robe, and items for an in-home facial. The basket is titled 'A Night-In with a Good Book.' As I move on to nearby silent auction items, I don't notice Tyson bidding on the book basket with his cell phone. He does the same for the winery tour, the Royals gift pack, then the in-home wine and painting class for twelve people I spent time admiring.

He introduces me to couples and colleagues from time to time. We continue to browse auction items, while gradually making our way into the dining room. Upon entering we view the displays for the live auction items. I cringe at the starting bid amounts listed on these items. A wide variety of vacations all over the world, a trip to The Super Bowl, a trip to The World Series, a trip to The Oscars, and a trip to The Grammy's are only a few extravagant items available for bidding.

At the end of the live auction items, several children ranging in age from five to eighteen man a raffle ticket table. "Would you like to purchase a raffle ticket for a chance to win a trip for two to Mexico for seven days; a day for four with the Royals to meet the players on the field during warm-ups, a photo op, and throw out the first pitch; or a new Honda CRV?" A teenage boy asks.

I look into the anxious faces of these children with diabetes and my heart answers for me. "Yes, I would like one ticket, please." I pull my debit card from my clutch to hand to a young girl at the table. Tyson attempts to push my hand back. He claims he will pay for my raffle ticket and his. "Uh-uh," I protest. "I'm lucky. If you purchase my ticket, it won't be my lucky ticket." I smile his direction.

"Seriously?" He acts as if my reasoning is nonsense.

"I've won many times before. I plan to win tonight." I hand my debit card over. The one-hundred-dollar ticket is an expense I don't need; however, it's for a great cause. If I win, I will choose the vehicle and save myself several thousand dollars on replacing my car. I think of the money my little brother snuck to me for a newer vehicle. This will be a great use of some of those funds. I gladly accept my raffle ticket from the youngest child at the table and slip it into my clutch. Tyson purchases five, yes five raffle tickets. I merely shake my head at his donation.

"I have the winning ticket; you just wasted your money," I inform him. His sexy chuckle wakes every cell in my body.

Next, we make our way to our assigned table. Two other couples seated, smile at us. They greet Tyson by name. He introduces me to each couple as 'his girlfriend, Ali.' I attempt to hide my shock. We decided this is our first date. Since when do couples on a first date claim to be boyfriend/girlfriend?

Soon the program begins as dinner arrives. Tyson leans in and informs me the emcee is Mitch Holthus. He attempts to tell me who that is, but I let him know he's a Chiefs' announcer. "You know, we do get Chiefs' radio and occasionally TV broadcasts of games outside of the KC area." I lace my words with sarcasm.

We enjoy our table conversations with our fancy dinner and dessert. As the tables clear, Mr. Holthus begins the live auction by describing each item before the auctioneer quickly rattles off numbers with the bids sometimes rising to twice the item's value. It's easy to get caught up in the excitement. Half-way through the items, he announces they will draw the first winning raffle ticket. This winner may choose between the three prizes. The gentleman picks the Royals day at the ballpark. Tyson groans as that's the item he wished to win.

After three more live auction items, they announce the second raffle ticket drawn. 9-2-4-2-4-8-4. I read over my numbers one more time as Tyson announces it is the person before him in line. His eyes bug out when he remembers I'm that person. I stand, excitedly jumping up and down, screaming 'I won! I won!'

"This lucky lady may choose between the trip to Mexico or the new CRV," Mitch reminds the guests.

I yell at the top of my lungs. "I want the SUV!"

Tyson stands, sweeping me into a tight hug. He wears the biggest smile I've seen on him yet. He shares in my excitement. He's the only person in this room of over five-hundred that knows just how much I need a different vehicle.

A young man hands me my new keys with a card explaining how I can claim my prize after the event. I pull him in for a quick hug–I catch him off guard. I thank him several times before he escapes the vicinity of our table.

Our tablemates laugh at my excitement. As the next auction items are announced, a toast rises to my good luck, and our table of eight sip our wine to celebrate.

"You were right; I can't believe your luck," Tyson whispers into my ear while twisting a strand of my hair around his fingers. "I am sorry, I tried to pay for your ticket earlier."

I squeeze his hand upon his thigh to express my acceptance of the apology. I've already forgotten all about it.

While waiting for all of the other prizes to be given away, mentally, I realize I still have $4,900 to use on sales tax, licensing, and insurance fees. I'll have some money left over, too. Maybe Clay can help me sell Gertrude for a couple hundred more dollars. I could purchase a new sofa for Jack's next visit to my apartment.

CHAPTER TWENTY

Ali:

Safely within the black sedan once again, Tyson holds my hand on the seat between us. I notice he didn't inform the driver of our destination upon entering. Did he arrange our next stop before picking me up this afternoon? My mind boggles at the infinite places we might be heading to now.

He catches me staring at him. "What are you thinking?"

I try to shake him off with no luck. "I don't like surprises," I inform him. "As long as I can remember, I have detested them." I smile at the memories of my mother's disdain for this fact.

"Did you enjoy the gala?"

"Of course, I did. I didn't like the impromptu shopping trip or your whisking me away to parts unknown." I extend my arm in front of us.

"It seems I owe you another apology. I..." He pauses running his hands down his face. "I... My mind runs away with itself when it comes to you. I get caught up in the excitement of being with you; I can't help myself." He shrugs apologetically. "I've never been impulsive. It is a new emotion for me. Please forgive me."

I nod acceptingly. "Where are you taking me now?" I hope to gently remind him he's attempting to surprise me yet again.

"It is early," he nervously states. "What are you in the mood for?" His eyes scan mine seeking answers in their depths.

"This is new to me. I don't date. I'm not sure how to or where to..."

Tyson slides closer to me in the leather seats, his hands secure both of mine, with our eyes locked, he silently assures me it's okay. My inexperience in Kansas City didn't detour him. "I am not ready for this night to end," he confesses. "I don't want to share your attention with others anymore this evening." He seems flustered by his desires.

"We could go to your place," my weak voice suggests. Processing my own words, I frantically attempt to reword them. "I mean," Crap! I need him to understand. "I'd like to continue our date, too. We could visit while we watch a movie or something. I didn't mean to insinuate..."

"Nor did I," he quickly states.

I hope he means it. Although we've hung out a few times while I worked at the firm, this is our first real date. There's so much we don't know about each other, I'm just not ready to jump in head first. I'm not like my friends or the women in my romance novels. Sweeping me off my feet doesn't equate to our naked bodies entwined in one another. I need a deeper emotional connection to open my deepest desires. I don't have a five-date rule, nothing is set in stone. It's a fluid concept that develops differently with each guy I date. I'm not a prude; I enjoy making out.

Tyson informs the driver of our new destination. I lean my head on his shoulder. As much as I am enjoying our evening, Clay still enters my thoughts. I need to talk to him tomorrow. I'll use the topic of selling Gertrude to start our conversation. I need to tell him about my date with Tyson. He needs to hear it from me. As the three of us tend to hang out, I feel a mutual interest in both Tyson and Clay. Tyson made the first move. It's not a competition. I hope my friendship and partnership with Clay will not be affected by this. I need to speak to him face to face to ensure we will be okay.

Soon, Tyson escorts me into his elevator, enters the code for the penthouse, and we are lifted high above the streets below. The close quarters feel electric with our expectations. I glance at him in my periphery. Tyson stares straight ahead. His anxious thumb beats a cadence against his thigh. I feel my heart pound heavy against my chest and my palms dampen as my pulse races.

When the ping announces our arrival, Tyson returns his palm to the small of my back, allowing me to enter a half-step ahead of him. *Now what?* I feel I should say something to break the tension. *Should I walk to the kitchen or the sofa? What are we to do now?*

"Let's get a drink." Tyson's words break through.

He leads me to the kitchen island barstools. Sliding one out, he helps me to climb onto it in my formal attire. I place my clutch to the side. As he extracts two water bottles from the refrigerator and prepares two glasses of red wine, I notice the counter displays a variety of sweets on a decorative cake stand. Come to think of it; the two wine glasses were setting in wait on the granite, too. *Had he predicted this ending to our date?*

As he places the water bottle and glass of wine in front of me, he scans my face. "I have a meat and cheese platter if you're hungry."

"I could nibble," I confess with a tilt of my head.

A slender wooden platter decorated with three types of cheese and two types of meat joins me at the island. Next napkins, plates, and mini forks are near me. Tyson chooses to stand across the marble island top from me. I select meat and cheese, then extend it to him. His eyes light and his dimples display themselves for me. Oh, the things those dimples do to my belly and my breathing. He slowly consumes my proffered delights. In between bites we smile.

"Okay, we need to snap out of this." I attempt to return us to our easiness from earlier. Just because we're in his apartment near his bedroom, doesn't mean we can't act as we have many times before. The fact that this is our first date shouldn't change our dynamic. "Truth time. Did you plan to return here tonight, or did you have a few options ready for the end of the date?"

Tyson chuckles at my keen observations. "I had three possible endings. One was a piano bar, and another was a walk on The Plaza." He shrugs his shoulders and quirks his mouth to the side. "I wanted us to be able to talk as our evening together winded down." I like his style. He's a planner—this proves his impulsiveness is, in fact, new to him.

"Can you believe I won a new car tonight?"

"About that," Tyson pulls out his cell phone. "Shouldn't we call Clay and share your good news?"

I'm surprised by this idea. We are on a date, Clay is our friend, but should this be how he learns about us?

Sensing my hesitation, Tyson rescues me. "I told Clay yesterday about your spa day with Marcia and our attending the JDRF Gala tonight," he explains.

So, Clay knew we were on a date. I worry about my friend and business partner. Is he alone at home tonight?

"Let's text him. If he's available, he can call us. If not, we can share later," Tyson states as his fingers fly over the buttons of his phone. His phone instantly signals an incoming FaceTime call.

"Well, let me see her," Clay orders of Tyson. Switching the camera mode to include me Tyson gleams with pride. "Hi, Ali."

"Hey," I greet back.

"Stand up—I can't see your dress for the countertop," Clay demands.

I clumsily step down from the stool and away from the kitchen island. After a moment, I reward Clay with a slow spin to get the full effect of my new outfit.

"What did you think of the jewelry we picked out?" Clay asks.

My hand caresses the teardrop diamond at my throat. "You helped?" I can't believe what I'm hearing. Oh my god, Clay knowingly helped Tyson prepare for our first date.

"It was my idea," Clay brags. Tyson's nod confirms it. "We looked at way too many earrings and necklaces. But when Tyson found those he knew they were the ones immediately." Blushing a bit at Clay's information, Tyson announces I have exciting news to share.

I pull my new car keys from my clutch complete with a Honda keychain and dangle them in front of the lens. "I bought a raffle ticket tonight and won a brand-new Honda CRV." My humongous smile makes its way back to my face. I've smiled so much tonight my cheeks ache.

Clay can't believe my luck. I share the story of Tyson attempting to purchase my raffle ticket and my informing him of my luck. After his excitement wanes a bit, I ask if he might be able to help me sell Gertrude. He agrees I should be able to get a couple hundred for her.

"I'm glad you called me to share your news, but the two of you are on a first date. You shouldn't be wasting your time talking to me," Clay teases.

"Stop," I demand.

"I'll see ya about game time," Tyson reminds Clay, and we disconnect.

We nibble on a few more sections from the meat and cheese platter before Tyson returns it to the fridge and refills our wine glasses.

"I'm ready to get out of this suit," he announces.

Jealousy washes over me. I'm ready to slip out of my new dress and heels—I was ready an hour ago.

"Your clothes from the spa are in the guest room." Tyson's words don't compute. *My clothes? How? When?* "I arranged for Marcia to drop them off here. I figured you could pick them up when we watched the game tomorrow if we didn't head back here tonight."

Tyson thought of everything. I'm impressed. Although I don't appreciate the surprises, I have to admit he planned a great first date down to the last detail.

"Impressed?" He asks knowingly. His sexy grin and dimples are back. I want to cross the distance between us and smother him with my lips.

"So, the guest room..." I repeat as I walk down the hall. I can hear his footsteps following close behind. I wave as I close the bedroom door. Safe inside, I lean against the door. Moments from tonight swim in my mind. The sound of Tyson's master bedroom door closing urges me back to the present.

I take my time changing into my t-shirt and shorts. I leave my flip-flops with my dress, heels, and jewelry on the bed. Opening the door, I notice the master bedroom door still shut. I make my way back to the kitchen to snag my water, before getting comfy on the sofa and flipping through channels on the large flat screen. I stop flipping on an eighties comedy about kids in Beverly Hills.

Tyson returns moments later in running shorts and a V-neck t-shirt. He secures more beverages with the dessert platter and he places them on the table in front of us.

For the next two hours, we talk about everything and nothing. Tyson makes me laugh. Eventually, I'm exhausted; I look at my phone it's one a.m.

Tyson catches me peeking. "It's late. You could stay in the guest room tonight." His hopeful gaze meets mine. "I promise to be on my best behavior." He holds up the Boy Scout Sign.

My mind drifts to a young Tyson attending pack meetings, earning his badges, doing good deeds, and camping. I'm sure he looked handsome in his uniform. Warm hands on my arms interrupt my thoughts.

"Where'd you go just now?" He asks.

"To thoughts of you in Boy Scouts." I smile sheepishly.

"I can't tell a lie," he states. "I was never a Boy Scout."

This doesn't surprise me. Tyson seems too citified to be a scout. "Do you have any photos of you as a boy?" I speak the words before I think them through.

Tyson pulls an album from beneath the TV. "Place your right hand on it," he directs. "Now, repeat after me. I promise I will honor these photographs, by not teasing, or posting on social media." I obey by repeating every word. Content with my promise, he relinquishes the album.

I gently open the thick cover to find everything from newborn pictures to several years of first-day-of-school pictures. Most photos included Tyson's proud big brother Stephen holding him or standing by his side. My fingers brush over his face. He flashes his dimples in every picture. In many ways, he resembles his nephew, Joe. Tyson was tall and skinny until his teen years when he filled out.

"I bet you had all the girls chasing after you."

Tyson pulls the album from my lap. I guess my trek down memory lane is over. "I was into sports and academics; I rarely wasted time with girls."

"I call bullshit!" His laughter fills my heart with joy. I dial Clay on my cell.

126

"What's up? Is the date over?" Clay asks in a lazy voice leading me to believe he's lying down.

"Sorry to bother you but I need intel," I announce. "Tyson claims he was much too busy with athletics and academics to and I quote 'waste time on girls.'"

Clay laughs so loud and hard; I must pull the phone away from my ear. Tyson mouths 'he lies' to me while we wait for Clay's laughter to subside.

"Guy code ties my hands on this one Ali," Clay explains through his laughter. "Tell Tyson I can't wait to see him this afternoon."

As I return my phone to the table, I shoot daggers to Tyson. "I'll have to ask Stephen or your parents," I inform him. "I will get to the bottom of this. I promise."

I find an action movie starring Bruce Willis for us to watch, while Tyson snags two more water bottles from

the fridge. I sink deeper into the sofa and throw pillows. Tyson throws a blanket over my legs upon his return.

"This is my favorite movie," he claims.

I can only roll my eyes, as this is every guy's favorite movie. I like the movie, but I don't quote it at every chance I get. "I heard somewhere that Ode to Joy appears over 20 times in this movie." Tyson shakes his head. "That makes it a Christmas movie." Guys hate it when girls claim this is a Christmas movie as if that detracts from the action.

Somewhere mid-movie, I drift off to sleep. Tyson does, too. When the bright morning sun bursts through the massive wall of windows, I try to use my arm to block it out. I move, Tyson stirs, then I groan as I sit up.

"Mornin' sleepy head," Tyson greets.

"I guess I didn't make it to the guest room."

Tyson chuckle is cut off by the ping of the elevator. Our eyes lock in fear.

"Good morning!" Clay calls as he steps off the elevator. "I thought you might be in need of coffee and breakfast."

I peek over the back of the sofa at him. Tyson walks to Clay as my mind comes to life. *Did Clay assume I would spend the night? Did he think I would sleep with Tyson on our first date? I hope he doesn't think I am easy.*

"Clay?" I call to him.

He kneels at the back of the sofa to speak to me. "I drove by your place to pick you up for a surprise breakfast at nine. Your car wasn't there, and you didn't answer the door. I took a chance you would be here." He taps me on the tip of my nose.

"I fell asleep watching *Die Hard,*" I confess trying to prove nothing happened last night.

"It's not the first time you've fallen asleep here." He brushes off the fact.

I can't believe Clay seems okay with our first date. He looks okay with the fact I spent the night here. Yes, I'd stayed here before, but Clay was here then, too. I still worry about the dynamic between the three of us. I need alone time with Clay.

"I have your favorites," he taunts waving the bakery bag from my favorite grocery store in front of my face.

The three of us gather around the kitchen island. Clay hands out coffee, Tyson passes out saucers, and Clay places donuts on each. I feel like a fish out of water. Once very comfortable in the company of these two men, now I worry.

"So, will there be a second date?" Clay asks the two of us.

My eyes nearly pop out of my head. Tyson only nods his head at his friend. I'm at a loss for words. Yesterday morning I woke up having feelings for the two men across from me. Feelings I didn't explore, nor did they. Feelings that led me to believe both reciprocated my interests. Last night, Tyson made his move, and I worried about Clay. Today, Clay is here acting as if Tyson taking me on a first date is the best thing. I must have misread my connection to Clay.

Tyson excuses himself to answer his cell phone. Clay places his hand on mine on the counter. "Did you have fun at the gala?"

I reply I won a free car how could I not have fun. Clay squints his eyes trying to read more from me.

"He planned this date for over a week," Clay divulges. "We talked about you a lot in the past week. He's got it bad for you."

I look at the ceiling. *How do I respond to that? How do I ensure Clay and I will remain friends and partners?* I look down the hallway to gauge how much time we might have before Tyson returning.

"I need you as a business partner," Clay confesses. "As business partners, we can be friends." He pushes a strand of hair from my forehead. I am sure my

bedhead looks lovely. "I helped him plan the surprise date and encouraged him to act on his feelings for you."

Did he just admit he stepped aside? He gave Tyson permission to act on his feelings. Clay wants to keep me as a business partner and friend, thus helped Tyson plan the perfect first date. *Should I leave it alone or confront Clay and Tyson? Do I need to know how they decided that Tyson won me? Does it matter to me?*

"For future reference, I detest surprises," I inform Clay.

Clay waves his palms back and forth in front of me. "The surprises were all him. I told him to ask you out. He worried you wouldn't accept as he was a former boss and my friend." Clay blows out a breath through his flattened lips. "Listen, he was very nervous. Give him a second date. Tell him no more surprises. He's worth a second chance."

"I am so confused," I state. "I woke up yesterday unsure exactly where I stood with Tyson and with you." I lick my lips. "Last night, Tyson made his move. I worried about you. I worried if I allowed myself to go on a first date with him, it might hurt us." A frustrated sigh escapes. "Today, I woke to you finding us asleep on the sofa after our first date. I am not sure..."

Clay rises to stand beside me. He wraps his arm around my shoulders and squeezes. "You and I are close friends and business partners. I would do anything for you. You've gone on a date with my best friend, and I hope it will lead to many more dates." He moves my chin to face him. "We are good. I promise."

I rise from the stool to wrap my arms around him. Clay returns the hug. I hope he spoke honestly just now. I need his friendship, I need my job, and by letting myself open up to the possibility, I think I have deep feelings for his best friend.

Still, in his arms, I ask, "He was a player in high school, wasn't he?"

Clay's loud laughter fills the penthouse. He pulls away from me and pretends to zip his lips and throw away a key. "How did that topic come up last night?"

I explain the Boy Scout comment, my picturing him as a child, and the photo album making its appearance. Of course, Tyson picks this moment to return to the living room.

"We will have two more joining us for the game today." He announces. "Stephen and Marcia need to visit a friend at the hospital, so Laila and Joe will be here soon." Tyson senses he missed an important conversation. "Everything okay out here?"

"May I use your guest shower? I can't look like this when they arrive." Tyson tells me to make myself at home. Clay insists my hair never looked better. I flip him off on my way down the hallway.

I'm roughing it today—I lay my clothes from yesterday morning on the bathroom vanity. I realize I took them off when I arrived at the spa in the morning and didn't wear them to the gala either. So, technically they are still mostly clean.

I place a towel on the hook, pull the shower door closed, then turn on the faucet. When the water warms my fingers, I pull the lever to change to the rain shower head above. As is my habit, I hop back with fear of cold water until the pipes fill with warmer water. This time when I jump, I slip. My wet feet slide forward; my body falls backward. I let out a yelp as my head connects with the tile shelf.

Immediately, Tyson pounds on the bathroom door. "Ali, what happened. Are you alright?"

"Ya, I'm okay," I holler back. "Don't come in."

"What happened?"

"I slipped, bumped my head, but I am okay," I promise. I stand under the spray and attempt to speed through my shower. I fear the longer I take; they might

barge in full of concern. I feel a goose egg growing where I hit my head.

When I emerge, freshly showered, Tyson's bedroom door is shut. I make my way to the kitchen. Clay's nowhere to be found. I look all around the space and into the dining area.

"He ran to pick up snacks for the kids," Tyson calls from the hallway. We meet at the end of the kitchen island. "Where did you hit when you fell?" His eyes perform a quick inspection head to toe for evidence. I point to the left side of my head. "Hop up here." Tyson points to the island top. I lift myself up; he places hands on my hips to assist. He deftly presses fingertips in my scalp, moving until he feels the bump. His hand shoots from my scalp at my hiss and wince. He places an ice pack in my left hand, ordering me to hold it to my bump. He remains close with a tender smile.

"There was something I should have done last night, that I will forever regret not doing," Tyson confesses as my brow furrows. "We didn't share our first kiss." His eyes scan for my reaction. I give him a slight nod. He tangles his hands gently in the back of my hair. I lean to him as he bends to me. He tilts his head slightly to the left. He begins with a gentle peck at the corner of my lips. My breath catches in my throat in anticipation of more.

His hot, plump lips massage mine, his teeth nip slightly; then he soothes the area with his lips again. His tongue grazes my lower lip seeking access. I part mine, and his tongue explores. Our tongues tango, our lips lavish, and our hands hold on tight.

Too soon Tyson leans his forehead to mine, as we fight for breath. "We should have done that last night," I whisper between pants. With impeccable timing, the elevator signals Clay's return with heavy laden arms full of goodies for the kids.

"What did you do to Ali?" Clay demands slinging the bags onto the counter before rushing over to me. I

hope he refers to my ice pack and not my heavy breathing.

"Nothing," Tyson defends.

"I fell in the shower," I explain. Two heads tilt and four eyes seek a full explanation. "I am a klutz. You've witnessed that before. When I pulled the lever for the shower to start, I hopped back to avoid the cold spray. I slipped and bonk." I point to the ice pack on my head.

"Why would you hop?" Clay probes.

"Because the first water out will be the cold water left in the pipes. I always jump back in fear. Don't you?"

"I turn the shower on for a while before I get in," Tyson states. "Problem solved."

"But I don't want water to spray all over the bathroom," I argue.

"You close the curtain," Clay says matter-of-factly.

"You must be careful with the curtain when you step in, but there shouldn't be any mess," Tyson explains.

I shrug them off. Surely it can't be as simple as they make it sound. They're used to the shower being separate from the tub. That's different. I question my practices and thought processes. Perhaps my jumping to avoid the first shower spray is something I can fix. If I can prevent the fear that hits me as I pull the shower lever each day, I will be much happier. My showers will be a calm, stress-free zone as they should be.

CHAPTER TWENTY-ONE

Tyson:

Tyson: game at my place tonight?
Clay: U Bet
Tyson: C ya @ 6

While watching the Royals game, I decide it was time to chat with Clay. "What are your plans for your grandpa's place?"

I catch him off guard. Clay moves to face me. "I haven't gotten around to that area yet. Why?"

Last night I remembered Clay's grandfather lived in the second story above the gym in a large loft. When his parents gifted the gym to him, they spent half a day upstairs gathering the belongings they wanted to keep of his grandfather. Clay couldn't bring himself to enter the private space. He was close to his grandpa and wasn't ready to face the memories.

I fidget in my chair before replying. "I thought, if you didn't have a plan for it, Ali might live there." I search Clay's face for any hint of a reaction. "I figured you eventually would rent out the space. If she rented, it would save you the hassle of advertising, showing the space, and screening the applicants." Clay nods. "I could help you prepare the space. We could rent a storage locker for the items you wanted to keep."

"I like the idea," Clay finally confesses, saving me from my rambling. "Do you think she would move? You know how independent she tries to be."

I chuckle. "Spin it, so she thinks she is doing you a favor. Let's get it cleaned out and ready. Then you can mention it as if her moving in would save you time and money finding a tenant." I tried to think it all through in detail in order to persuade my friend.

CHAPTER TWENTY-TWO

Ali:

Tyson fixes a delicious dinner for us this evening at his penthouse. I admit he makes me self-conscious of my lack of cooking skills. He learned from his mother. He claims she liked the children to help her often in the kitchen. I make a mental note to thank her when I see her next.

"Perhaps you could give me cooking lessons sometime," I playfully suggest while we load the dishwasher together. "I might be a lost cause, but it could be fun."

"I am sure you are a great cook. You just need the right motivation to spark your desire for cooking," he claims placing the last fork into the bin, shutting the door, and turning on the dishwasher.

Am I his spark of desire for this meal? Tyson teaching me to cook sounds better by the minute. There's something about a man confident in the kitchen that sparks a fire inside my core. Not just any man, Tyson in the kitchen, is very sexy.

Tyson's strong hands splay on my hips, turning me towards him. "You like the idea of cooking with me, don't you?" I nod biting my lower lip. "Let's plan on cooking together on Saturday," he suggests. Again, I nod.

Tyson's lips sweep mine. His fingers tighten at my waist digging into my skin. I feel his need as he attempts to hide it. I feel the same need, desire, and want. I moan as his tongue finds entry into my mouth. Our tongue tango further fuels my flames. With no warning, he lifts me to sit on the island top, never breaking our kiss.

My fingertips slowly slide from his shoulders to his spectacular pectorals. His workouts mold every inch of him into a hard-sculpted Adonis. Continuing their decent next they play over the ridges of his abdominals. I recall viewing these ridges while Clay joined him in the ring at the gym. I clutch him, needing his strength to center me as I feel I'm falling into a canyon.

Tyson places his forehead on mine. His fingers slip under the hem of my shirt. My abdominals tense at the sensation of his skin touching mine. His eyes search mine for permission. I've fantasized about his touch many times—the reality is more than I dreamed. His brown eyes dilate in front of mine, while his hands climb up my stomach to my breasts. I long for no barrier between us as his fingertips trace the lacey edges of my bra. I whimper and his eyes close tight. He lifts his head from mine as he removes my T-shirt.

I lick my lips nervously under his gaze. My breasts heave with each intake of breath. His eyes pinned on my chest, his breath quickens, and his nostrils flare. Slowly he slides his eyes to mine. In their melted chocolate depths, I fall under his spell. I want what he wants, I need what he needs, and my desires match his.

In a moment of sheer bravery, I reach behind my back, and unfasten my bra. Tyson wastes no time in sliding the strap off each shoulder. My nerves catapult sky-high. I'm always self-conscious of my tiny breasts. I know men tend to be a breast or butt guy, I find myself hoping Tyson prefers asses. Maybe then, my just shy of handful mounds won't turn him away.

His fingers tiptoe up to my ribcage. Each inch they climb prickles my skin more—I love this. Don't get me wrong; my toys work just fine, it's just not the same, I miss a male's touch and my reaction to it.

I miss the additional stimulation of all my senses, having a hard-male body brings.

Tyson grasps my wrist, raising my arm straight into the air. Seated on the kitchen island, this seems odd until his other hand traces the script of my tattoo. I suck in a sharp breath between my teeth. No one has ever seen them.

"What does it mean?" Tyson whispers still tracing the script.

I raise my other arm. Tyson runs his fingers over another tattoo.

"Carpe Diem," he reads aloud. He places his left hand on my tattoo along my ribcage, under my right breast. "Seize," Then he places his right hand on my left tattoo, "the day."

I nod, his hands remain on my ribs while his thumbs lightly graze under each breast—it's more than I can take. I whimper.

"I like them," he states, cupping each breast with a grin. "And, I like these." He growls, squeezing them before pinching each nipple.

A muffled plea escapes as I arch into his touch. I need more—I desire all of him. I've been avoiding intimacy, but now I welcome it. "Tyson please," I plead.

His lips envelope mine. We devour each other sucking, nipping, and licking. I'm fevered. Every inch of my flesh burns. Every cell craves more. This man is everything to me. For the last two weeks, we've dated and learned about each other. To some we are moving too fast. I've found my soulmate. When I look into his sexy brown eyes, I see my soul reflected back at me. There is no doubt in my mind, we are meant to be together. I moved to Kansas City instead of St. Louis, I chose an apartment in Liberty over all other suburbs in this large city, I applied at the temp agency instead of taking a clerk or waitress job, I received placement at the Lennox Law Firm...everything happens for a reason. Tyson brings out the best in me, I hope I do the same for him.

He throws me over his right shoulder. I clutch his butt as he swats mine on our way to his bedroom. I bounce when thrown onto his bed. He deftly removes my shorts and panties. I lift myself up on my elbows, sucking on my lower lip as I witness Tyson strip, nude in front of me.

Damn my man is fine. I've fantasized about him for months now. Since our first date, my nightmares disappeared. They have been replaced by hot fantasies involving Tyson. Although I could feel him through his clothes, the sight before me is more perfect than I dreamt. He could be a model, made into a sculpture, be a movie star—instead he is mine. I want to lick and taste every inch of him. I long to hear him call my name at climax.

He slinks slowly over my body, as I tremble in anticipation. His hands plant on either side of my head, a wicked grin on his face. Leaning down to kiss my lips, his curly hair tickles my pubis. I reach between us, not breaking our kiss, to stroke him. A moan of pleasure escapes, at the velvety soft skin on his rock-hard cock heavy in my hand. I've never held one before, but I instinctively know what to do. I slowly stroke him base to tip, swirl over the head, then repeat the motion. He pulls away from our kiss. His closed eyes and labored breathing ensure I am indeed doing this right.

"Ali," he groans his lips brushing mine. "I need to be inside you."

"Yes, please," I beg. I position him at my entrance. As I guide his shaft, he slowly thrusts inside inch by inch. The overwhelming feeling of fullness is more than I can bare. I place my palms on his tight ass, my fingers digging in, and squeeze as I moan his name.

He curses, quickly pulling out. He rummages in his bedside table, as he stands gloriously naked just out of my reach. I admire his heavy cock, as he tears open a foil packet and rolls it on. When his arms return to the bed, I pull him over me. His eyes bore into mine as he once again makes his way into the deepest part of me.

Tyson pauses his movements sensing my need. "Okay?"

I nod, breathing through clenched teeth. "Slow please."

He doesn't pull out, but grinds himself into me. The exquisite friction shoots sparks in my core. "S-H-I-T," I slowly shout with pleasure. My hands on his ass encourage him to continue.

He begins to rock in and out, with a delicious grind after every penetrative thrust. I feel a coil tighten deep in my core.

I whisper, "yes," a second before he completely withdraws.

"I'm not going to last long," he growls, before parting my thighs, his head diving in. My head flies back causing my chest to jut forward when his hot wet lips suckle my clit. He licks, and sucks then blows his cold breath over my folds. When he returns his mouth to my nub, two long fingers thrust inside. They tickle a very sensitive spot for only a moment before I explode, moaning his name. Ever muscle in my body tightens, hot needles prick everywhere, as white lightning bolts burst behind my closed eyelids.

Tyson thrusts inside in one quick movement. I feel my muscles grip him in waves of my pleasure. He rapidly pistons into me, groaning as he nears his own release. I slowly come down from my orgasm as he thrusts deeply once more, grinding against me, growling my name at his release.

He pulls my back into his chest and places one leg over mine. We cuddle in silence recovering from our high.

"I love you," he murmurs near my ear.

I'm unable to respond. Tears well up, clogging my throat. I tightly squeeze his arms at my belly. Many quiet moments pass.

"You're amazing," he murmurs.

"So, I did okay?"

Confused by my words, Tyson turns my body to face his.

"I'm um..." I nervously clear my throat. I remind myself that I love him, and he loves me. I am safe in his arms, I can share this with him. "I'm not very experienced," I blurt, covering my face with my hands.

"You weren't a vir..."

"No! I'm not a virgin, I just...I've only been with..." I stammer.

"Ali," Interrupting, Tyson pulls my hands from my face, kissing each one before releasing them. "You were perfect. It's all about feelings. You just let what you want and what feels good lead the way." He kisses the tip of my nose. "I'm in love with you, all of you. I don't care if you aren't very experienced. In fact, I kinda like that you aren't," he grimaces. "I don't want to think about you with other guys." His hand combs through my hair. "Just so you know, it felt so good, I believed you knew exactly what you were doing."

"But, you'll tell me if I do something wrong, won't you."

"I have only two rules I don't want you to break." He looks deep into my eyes. "No teeth on my cock, and no sex with anyone but me."

I grin. "I believe I can abide by those rules."

I place a peck on the corner of his mouth. He quickly pulls me in for a deeper kiss. This leads to roaming hands, which leads to orgasm number two and three, before we fall asleep in each other's arms.

***

Stretching in the early morning sunlight, I feel a pleasant ache in many muscles I wasn't aware existed. I look to Tyson's pillow to find he isn't in bed. Craning my neck, I hear the sounds of his shower. I tiptoe into the master bath and slip inside the shower stall behind him.

"Good morning," he greets while lathering shampoo in his hair.

"I love you," I return as I join him under the rainfall-shower head as streams of water bathe us on all sides.

He wraps me tight in his arms, my chest slick against his soapy one. "I love you, too. How'd you sleep?"

"Very well," I reply.

After rinsing the suds from his hair, he wraps around me again and looks deep into my eyes. "I lost control with you last night," he confesses.

"I didn't mind." I grin and glide my soapy hands over his shaft, enjoying its growth at my touch. Using both hands in my ministrations, I enjoy Tyson's head thrown back, eyes closed, and moans escaping. I pull his neck toward me, when our eyes meet, I beg him to take me now. I can't wait another minute. Fortunately, Tyson does the thinking for us both, he insists we rinse off and move to the bedroom near the condoms before we continue.

CHAPTER TWENTY-THREE

Ali:

It's moving day! I spring from my bed excited to start my new life in a much larger space. Since I rented this apartment furnished, all my items will fit in Tyson's SUV in one trip. I box up my bedding. After I dress, I box up my pajamas and makeup. I look at the clock. The guys won't be here for an hour. Ugh. What should I do?

I take a selfie by my boxes and text it to Jack. He won't be up yet, but I want him to see the stages of my move. He tried to find a reason to come up to help me move but it didn't work out with his ball schedule. Next, I skim through social media apps to see what everyone is up to in Hannibal.

The guys burst through my door thirty minutes early. Thank goodness. I'm too excited to sit any longer. We swiftly load the boxes, leave the keys on the counter as the landlord instructed, lock the door, and drive away.

My nerves go into overdrive, as Tyson parks the SUV behind the gym. We have four assigned parking spots just off the alley with a metal roof covering them and my first door is on ground level. Clay hands me my new keys, suggesting I open and hold the door as they unload the boxes. I skip over, insert the key in the door, and sigh happily when it opens. I use my key again to open the door at the top of the stairs, grinning like a loon as they place my boxes against an empty wall.

I take in my new place. Clay insisted on leaving furniture until I purchase my own. They don't know it yet, but I will suggest we buy an item or two this afternoon. Though the sofa is older than I had at my old place, it's in much better condition. My new space is huge. I spin around amazed that I get to call this home.

Peeking out the large window, I watch the guys gather more boxes. I can't believe how lucky I was the day Gloria told me of my two new placements. The following Monday, my life started on a new path. Little did I know, I would gain two new friends, a boyfriend, financial security, and a new apartment.

"Thanks for holding the doors for us," Clay blusters while placing three more boxes on my stack.

"I'm sorry, I was just enjoying my new apartment space."

With all of my boxes carried up, we head out for pizza and a few items I need to purchase.

Tyson: U home?
Me: Yes
Tyson: come open door
Me: OK

I rush down to let Tyson in. He swings the door open wider than necessary. I ask why he dropped by as I begin to ascend the stairs. When he doesn't reply, I turn. He's still holding the door open with a humongous grin.

"Apache, come," Tyson speaks firmly.

I don't believe my eyes when the dog bounds up the stairs to greet me. Tyson shuts the outer door and follows. I can't speak. I can't process it. I quickly open the apartment door allowing the three of us to enter.

Tyson rescues me from my struggle to speak. "I borrowed Apache for the day." He kneels to pet the dog. "We must have him home by nine tonight."

I sit on my wooden floor; Apache immediately lathers me with kisses to my face, neck, and ears as he lies atop me on the floor. I giggle until my sides ache and Tyson assists me to a sitting position again. Apache lies in front of me with his paw on my knee, while Tyson fixes him a bowl of cold water. "What brought this on?" I ask Tyson.

He explains the two of us got on so quickly at the park; he thought a play date would be a fun idea. He remembered the guy's name from the park, he found his number on the internet and reached out. His eyes and smirk lead me to believe there is more to this story than he shares.

Our afternoon and evening pass quickly. We walk around the neighborhood, we go to the park, and then we drive Apache home. As we walk to the front door, I wish I didn't have to return him. I'd love to have a dog to keep me company. Tyson introduces me to Thomas when he opens the door. Apache remains by my side. It's awkward that he doesn't display excitement to see return to his owner. We are invited to make ourselves at home in the living room. Apache lies near my feet. Tyson shares our adventures with Apache today while I absent-mindedly reach down to stroke Apache's back.

"Ali, Apache seems smitten with you," Thomas says. *Smitten? Who says smitten?* "Unfortunately, we don't seem to get along, so I am looking for a new home for Apache."

My breath catches in my throat. "I'm sorry to hear that," I whisper.

"Would you consider taking Apache for me? I need someone I can trust to care for him. I tried to honor his partner's death by caring for him, but we lost five of our brothers, I think our time together only reminds us of the pain." Thomas' voice breaks as he explains.

I could never imagine the horror of losing my team and being the lone survivor. It has to be much worse than my experience with Leslie. I read somewhere that service dogs suffer depression and a form of

PTSD just like humans in extreme situations. It's a shame these two can't heal one another.

"Ali?" Tyson urges me to return from my thoughts.

I smile down at Apache then pat my lap. Apache stands tilting his head from side to side to interpret my request. "Would you like to live with me?" I ask. Yes, I expect a reply from a dog. Apache sits then raises a paw to my knee. Looking to Thomas, I ask, "Can I say yes on a trial basis? I mean, it's a yes, a firm yes. However, if after a couple of days or a week Apache is miserable with me, can we discuss other options. I don't foresee any issues. He was perfect at my apartment and on our walks today," I ramble.

It's agreed that Apache will move in with me tonight. Tyson loads up the large dog crate and dog bed along with the bowls, food, leashes, and a basket of chew toys with bones. I receive a full military and veterinary history along with a typed 'Things to Know About Apache' list.

When we say our good-byes, I feel it in my bones that Apache will love being with me as much as I will with him. I thank Tyson repeatedly on the drive home. He confesses that he slipped his card to Thomas in the park that day stating we would be available if he needed a dog sitter. Thomas recently reached out to Tyson about this arrangement. All that matters to me is I now have a dog.

Tyson unloads Apache's items, while I walk him in the nearby grass. Tyson helps me arrange the dog paraphernalia around my space before saying good night. I hope my kiss conveys how much I appreciate his actions today. Our kiss deepens as Tyson's tongue enters my mouth. Apache lets out a low growl from our feet.

"Our first point of business it to teach Apache he must share you with me," Tyson whispers with his forehead on mine. I attempt to calm my breathing, pull away, and look down at Apache. "At least I can rest easy knowing he will protect you."

I step outside my apartment door and properly kiss Tyson good-bye. I thank him once more for arranging my new pet. When I slip back in, Apache anxiously waits for me.

As it's late, I change into a tank and shorts, brush my teeth, wash my face, then climb into bed. Apache shadows my every move paying close attention. He sits on the floor near my side of the bed. I pat beside me, but he doesn't join me.

"Apache, come," I order. He excitedly hops into the bed lying next to me. I pet him and speak to him about our day and our plans for tomorrow. I realize I'm carrying on a conversation with a dog. At least I'm not talking to myself. As I grow tired, I reposition myself to fall asleep. Apache stands on the bed, steps over me, and sprawls out on the other half of my king-sized bed. Thank goodness my new bed is enormous. Apache isn't a dainty dog—we both have plenty of room to spread out. I realize Thomas must not have shared his bed with Apache. I can't imagine forcing him to sleep on the floor in the corner. I hate spending most of my time alone and I want a dog to fill the void. I have no doubt Apache, and I will quickly fall into a comfortable routine with each other.

The next day, I invite Clay over via text. I don't know if Tyson had discussed the pet situation in Clay's apartment before we took Apache or not. I feel I need to address it with him. When he enters the apartment, Clay doesn't seem surprised to see Apache lying on the floor.

"How'd last night go?" Clay asks kneeling to pet my dog.

I explain our time last night and this morning to Clay. "I take it Tyson spoke to you about this ahead of time?" I ask.

"Yes, I thought it was a terrific idea. I like the idea of a strong male protecting you. The fact that Apache is military trained is a bonus in my book."

"I'll keep him in his crate, while I am at the gym. I'll take a break mid-morning and afternoon to let him outside and probably eat lunch up here, too."

Clay informs me I should bring Apache to work with me. He will buy another dog bed and water bowl for the office. I hedge at the idea until Clay explains Apache is trained to be in the presence of people at all times. He will behave, and it will be fun to have him around.

"I have the greatest boss in the world," I cheer. Clay quickly reminds me we are partners, and he is no longer my boss.

Clay and I take Apache on a long walk before he makes an excuse to leave. I call Tyson and share I get to take my dog to work with me. He already knows this fact but enjoys my excitement.

CHAPTER TWENTY-FOUR

Ali:

Weeks fly by. I love my time with my new projects at the gym. We've replaced the blacked-out windows and doors with new lighter advertising. I found images of boxing, kickboxing, of men, women and children that don't allow patrons on the sidewalk to see inside but let members inside see out. This lightened the interior space tremendously.

We have two new state of the art locker rooms. One for males and one for females. We now have two rings, a separate room to hold classes, two new water fountains that easily fill water bottles, a kid boxing league with 35 members and three teachers, two kickboxing classes with 30 enrolled in each, and private lessons now offered to members and the community.

Clay's father helped a former MMA fighter join our staff. He draws in a whole new member-base for us. He provides private instruction for members only. By making him available to members only, we are increasing our monthly membership just by offering this service.

We installed a new scan card entrance on the front door, raised the monthly membership rate by $10 and are now open 24 hours 7 days a week to members. We've recruited 50 new members in the past three months.

Our little gym is doing very well. Clay and I love what we do, helping others become fit, and providing a service to the community. Our work schedule is no longer 8-5 weekdays. We've hired some great trainers and instructors to assist in our services. I enjoy attending the six-a.m. kickboxing class three days a week. During event or class sign-ups I often work until 8 p.m. to allow those who work the opportunity to come in.

Clay assists with the kids boxing instruction on Saturday mornings and afternoons. He serves as the referee during their sparring matches on Sunday afternoons. Tyson serves as a judge and I am in charge of ringing the bell to end each round. Clay wanted me to wear a bikini and carry the large sign around the ring announcing the round number. Tyson quickly informed him that wasn't appropriate for an 18 and under league.

I'm currently working on connecting our league with two others in the KC Metro area. When I'm finished we will be able to box kids in other leagues instead of only within our own.

Apache has become something of a mascot for our gym. Everyone enjoys his presence especially the kids. I love the convenience of living upstairs from my work. I can sleep later and go home for meals without a long, stressful commute. Apache and I do spend many nights at Tyson's. This requires us to commute 25 minutes, which is still relatively low for the Kansas City area. I encourage Tyson to stay at my place the evenings before my early morning classes. He doesn't seem to mind slumming it in my apartment.

I love that he has wealth but appears very normal. Occasionally we attend fancy functions like the JDRF Gala, but usually we dine casually, go to movies, or relax at our apartments. From time to time, I have to put him in his place for attempting to purchase items for me. I remind him I have a steady income and I don't need him to provide for me.

It is important to me that I keep some of my independence. I believe this is what I gained from Leslie's tragedy. I am cognizant that

I enjoy hobbies of my own and do my own thing. I enjoy my relation-ship with Clay as a best friend and partner at work. I love Tyson and am very comfortable in our relationship. Both men understand my desire to not become so wrapped up in them that I lose my own iden-tity. I just have to remind them occasionally.

This week, I am feeling run-down. I skip my morning kickboxing classes. I nibble on crackers throughout the day as I feel nauseous. I fear I've caught a bug from one of our adorable kid boxers.

Tyson and I were going to a Royals game tonight, but I ask him to take Clay in my place. I only feel like resting on the sofa.

Clay: Have U talked to Ali lately?
Jack: 2 days ago, why?
Clay: She's been sick for over a week
Clay: She didn't feel like a Royals game, so I came with Tyson
Jack: I'll call tonight, thanks for heads up
Clay: No Prob

CHAPTER TWENTY-FIVE

Ali:

After a late dinner and a long walk with Apache, Jack calls. "Hey, little brother." I greet.

"How was your day?" He asks.

I share the updates we implemented at the gym. I promise to send him a picture of my new bookshelves and share several Apache stories.

"You sound tired," Jack notes.

"I am, I still don't feel well," I explain.

"Been to the doctor, yet?" He asks. I know it is his way of telling me I need to go.

"I have an appointment next week." I bite my thumbnail as I try to summon up the courage I need.

"Don't wait until next week. Why don't you go to urgent care tomorrow?"

"It's not the type of illness you take to urgent care," I hedge.

"Ali," I sense Jack's growing frustration in his voice. "There are only two types of illnesses: E.R. visit or urgent care visit. Which one is this?" His voice takes on a tone I'd often heard in my father's voice.

"It's an obstetrics type of illness," I state. The cat is officially out of the bag now.

"Obstetrics, as in O.B., as in pregnant?" Jack's raised voice worries me. I don't want my parents to hear him.

"Shh!" I whisper-hiss at him over the phone. "I don't want the whole world to know."

"So, you aren't sick—you're pregnant," he states processing my situation. "I bet Tyson is over the moon. Have you told Clay yet?"

"I just found out this morning. I took two pregnancy tests before work," I confess. "So, you are the only one I have told."

"Ali, you need to tell Tyson," he demands. "Unless he isn't the father..."

"Jack, of course, he is the father," I spit. "I just need to plan a creative way to share my news with him." I close my iPad on the coffee table. "In fact, I was searching on Pinterest for ideas when you called."

"Promise me you will tell him tomorrow."

"Jack, I will tell him. Let me spend some time on Pinterest, and I will text you later tonight. Okay?"

An hour later a horn honks three times; I look out the window to find Tyson climbing from his black SUV. I head down to open the door for him. Apache follows close on my heels—he senses the change in me. He's been glued to my side and overly protective when others approach me this week.

"Hey, gorgeous," Tyson greets as I open the outer door. He places a quick kiss on my forehead before prompting me upstairs.

I need to talk to Clay about installing a buzzer system, so I can press a button to allow people up to my apartment, then I wouldn't have to take the stairs so often. I'm exhausted and out of breath when I enter my apartment.

Tyson pulls his arm from behind his back and kneels behind me on the floor. Apache sits beside him. When I turn to face him, I find my man on his knees, a beautiful bouquet in his outstretched arm for me. I take the proffered flowers immediately inhaling their fragrance. My stomach lurches a bit at the sweet scents. I breathe through mouth to stave off nausea. Tyson remains on bended knee. Next, he opens a tiny black velvet box in his hands. My eyes take in the sparkling diamond before me. *It can't be. He can't be.* I look to Tyson's face for answers.

"Ali, will you marry me?" Tyson's masculine voice speaks the words every little girl dreams of hearing.

Tears fall from my eyes. My hands shake as I attempt to grasp the ring box. I pull them back to hide my shakiness, then cover my mouth with my hand, and dart for the bathroom. Of all the times to be affected by morning sickness, why did it have to be in the middle of my proposal? Several minutes pass before my stomach calms. Tyson stands outside the closed door asking to help in any way he can.

As I lean my head on the cold bathtub, I reminisce Tyson's proposal from minutes earlier. The man of my dreams proposed to me. He got down on one knee and asked me to marry him. My thoughts move to his possible reaction when I share I'm carrying his baby.

Wait!

This CAN'T be a coincidence.

I told Jack I was pregnant and an hour later, Tyson shows up and proposes. That little ass—Jack told Tyson. Tyson's only offering to marry me because he knocked me up. Another violent round of vomiting erupts. Tyson turns the knob over and over attempting to enter. There is nothing he can do.

Finally, I splash water on my face and brush my teeth before opening the door. Tyson's pained face greets me. I assure him I am fine on my way to get a bottle of water from the fridge.

After assuring I'm okay for the umpteenth time, Tyson announces, "You are killing me, Ali. I need an answer."

"I can't believe Jack called you." I shake my head in disbelief. "We don't have to do this. This isn't the sixties."

Hurt shows on Tyson's face. "Ali..."

"Listen, I am touched that you would offer to marry me, but I don't want us to rush to the altar."

Now he interrupts me. "Jack didn't call me. Why would he call me? And why do you think we would be rushing to the altar? I asked you to marry me not to elope. Our engagement can be as long or as short as you'd like."

"Let me see your cell phone," I demand. He slides it into my outstretched hand. I scroll through recent texts, recent calls, and deleted messages. I don't find evidence that Jack had contacted him after we spoke. I pass his phone back. I flee from the room, safe in the bathroom with the door locked; I dial my brother.

The moment he answers, I spit, "Why did you? How could you? I trusted you. I told you I needed one night. I only wanted one night to plan. But *NO*, you had to call your buddy Tyson and tell him. Seriously, Jack, I can't believe you would betray me like that. I needed time. I planned to tell him in my own way."

Jack shouts, yes shouts at me. "Ali Stop!" I heave an exasperated sigh. "I. Did. Not. Call. Anyone. I didn't text anyone. What are you so upset about?" He waits for my reply. When silence spans moments, he continues. "You need to calm down and think of your baby. Getting this worked up can't be healthy."

Leave it to my seventeen-year-old brother to be the voice of reason in my mess of a life. I attempt a few calming breaths to gather myself. "You promise you didn't tell Tyson?" I ask as my voice quivers. He vows he didn't. "Jack, I messed up big this time. I jumped to conclusions and ruined what should have been the happiest moment of my life." My brother offers words of assurance that it will all work out. He orders me to collect myself, apologize to Tyson; then I'm to call or text him later so that he can hear the entire story of tonight's events.

Calm and collected, I exit my bathroom. Tyson leans against the wall near the door, arms crossed, and worry written on his handsome face. Apache sits protectively beside his feet. At the sight of them, hiccupping sobs overcome me. I attempt to wipe the tears, but they flow too fast. "You promise Jack didn't tell you?" I plead between hiccups. Tyson carries me to the sofa.

"Babe you are scaring me." He pulls me onto his lap. Apache whines at my feet. "Does Jack know why you are sick? What is it? It's bad, isn't it." He plays with my hair while massaging my neck and scalp. It feels divine. "Whatever you have, we can fight it. I'll get you the best doctors."

"Tyson," I need to stop his worry. "I'm okay. Really." I promise while looking into his deep brown eyes. I gulp and wipe the last of my tears. "I told Jack, and you showed up within an hour. That's why I thought you were here." I run my hands down his jaws, over his strong shoulders, and stop on his muscular arms. I place a tender kiss on the corner of his mouth. "Before; I answer your charming proposal, I need to tell you something." I take a deep breath. "I'm pregnant." It comes out as timid a whisper.

"Pregnant?" Tyson repeats. "We're pregnant! You aren't dying of some rare illness—you're carrying my baby?" Every ounce of worry fades from his face and immediately I see excitement and love.

"So, you can see how I might have thought Jack called you, then worried you rushed to marry me given my current state."

"Oh my god!" Tyson bellows. "Yes, I see your train of thought. However, there is a major flaw in your logic. You see if I showed up here less than an hour after you spoke to Jack, I wouldn't have had time to pick up flowers and a ring." He grins pulling me tight to his chest. I inhale his scent. "I would have already had the ring, which would mean I planned to ask you before finding out about the baby." I push off his chest as I digest his words. If I weren't so scared at the moment, I would have slapped that smug grin from his gorgeous face.

"Whatever. It doesn't matter now." I wiggle on his lap. "Yes."

"Yes?" He parrots. "Yes, you will marry me. Hell Ya! We are getting married, and you are having my baby. I'm the luckiest man alive," he cheers and Apache barks loudly.

"Nope, I'm the luckiest woman alive."

His mouth attacks mine. His lips suck, and his teeth bite. His tongue asks for access, and I allow it to find mine. My head swims as he plunders my mouth. I have to pull back, resting my forehead on his, to catch my breath.

"I need to make a call," he murmurs interrupting our make-out session. I look questioningly into his molten brown depths. I like knowing I affect him as he affects me. "My parents knew I planned to propose at the Royals game tonight. I am sure they are staring at their phones anxiously awaiting my call," he explains.

"Was there any doubt I'd say yes?" I half-tease.

"When you ran to the bathroom for two long puking fits, even I began to doubt your answer."

"I'm sorry. At least we have a funny story to tell," I offer.

I rise from his lap as he calls his parents. It's a FaceTime call, so I hurry to right myself in the bathroom mirror.

"Finally." His father's deep voice answers.

"Mom, Dad, Ali and I have some news to share," Tyson begins as if they don't know why he's calling.

"Hi, Tyson," Stephen greets from behind his parents with Marcia at his side.

"Looks like the family is all there," Tyson states as Laila and Joe join the group. He motions me over to his side, wrapping his arm around my shoulders. "Ali and I are getting married."

Cheers and congratulations fly through the phone. Tyson's mom and Marcia wipe happy tears from their cheeks. Laila and Joe cheer louder than the others. Tyson turns my face to his and kisses me. Of course, his family cat-calls, ahh's, or acts disgusted by our display of affection.

When they request I relive his proposal—I leave out the vomiting and pregnancy announcement for now. His mom and sister inform me we must schedule a planning lunch sometime soon. Laila announces she wants to be our flower girl and tells Joe he'll be the ring bearer. Their excitement is contagious. We chat for a bit, then one by one we say our good-byes.

"I wanted to share all of our good news," Tyson confesses. Understanding what he means, I suggest we plan a dinner and share our good news face to face with the adults. He likes my idea.

I text Jack to call me if he can. Soon my phone rings. I share every detail of Tyson's proposal and my freak out before accepting. Jack laughs his butt off. Of course, the little shit finds my discomfort hilarious. I put him on speaker, and the three of us chat until he hears my parents in the hallway and needs to hang up. I don't let my thoughts drift to sharing my news with my parents. I will save that mess for another time. Tonight, I need to celebrate with Tyson

Next, Tyson calls Clay on speaker. After he congratulates us, he tells me he was worried Tyson might go ahead with the proposal with him at The Royals game. He teases about the kiss-cam. I laugh so hard I have to excuse myself to the bathroom. Clay lets us go, so we can celebrate.

As excited as I am, exhaustion hits me hard. I ask Tyson to spend the night. I interpret his sly grin as he planned for that. When he takes Apache out before bed and returns with a duffle bag, I can only giggle. We agree to discuss our future plans tomorrow.

As I prepare for bed, Tyson states we have another problem. I peek into the bedroom area to see Apache sprawled out on his side of the bed leaving half for Tyson and me to share. I suggest that we cuddle, and Tyson informs me it is crucial that we set boundaries sooner rather than later with Apache.

Tyson carries Apache's bed from the living room placing it on my side of the bed. As I crawl under the quilt, Tyson orders Apache to the floor then crawls in beside me. After licking my cheek, Apache snuggles into his bed without a whimper. Tyson murmurs something about being the man of the house to which I snicker. I know we will find three of us in the bed by morning.

I fall asleep to sweet thoughts of our family of three morphing into a family of four in the months to come. My thoughts are light. I don't dwell on when we will marry, where we will live, or if I will tell my parents—I leave the heavy thoughts for another time. Tonight, I sleep knowing I am safe, loved, and happy.

CHAPTER TWENTY-SIX

Ali:

Tyson: What time is dinner?
Me: evite stated 7 pm
Tyson: I should be done with court by 5
Me: 👍
Tyson: 😊
Tyson: 😑
Me: enough!
Tyson: Love You!
Me: Love ya

"Heading out soon?" Clay asks popping his head through my office door.

"Ya, you still coming at six?" I remind him.

"Of course, I've got you covered," he promises. "Now get out of here. Take a nap before chaos ascends tonight."

Apache and I stop by my apartment for a few items, then drive to Tyson's. His new doorman balks at a strange dog visiting the penthouse unannounced. I can't call Tyson as he's in court. I pull up my texts from earlier to show proof I have talked to him today. Then I pull up two selfies we took with Apache in the park to prove Tyson knows my dog. Still a little skeptical I assure him I know the current code to the penthouse elevator, then proceed to enter the elevator. If he has a problem with it, he can call Tyson. Apache sits touching my leg as the elevator lifts us high above the city.

Tyson took pity on my limited cooking skills, limited time, and constant morning sickness—he arranged for chef to prepare our meal tonight. He wants me to relax after work before our exciting announcement. As I prepare for a bath, I set the alarm on my phone for five-fifty. In case I fall asleep later, this will allow me to be up before the others arrive. I start a warm bath, light a few candles Tyson bought for me, and sync my playlist with his Bluetooth speakers.

I sigh as I slip one foot then the other into the warm water. Usually, my bath would be hot, but I think that might not be safe for the baby. I need to purchase some parenting books soon I have a lot to learn. I slowly lower myself into the oversized tub filled near the top. I press the jacuzzi button activating multiple jets. Oh, my! This is heaven. The sound of the jets brings Apache in to assess my safety. Everything seems okay, so he flops on the tile floor near the tub. I sing along with my favorite songs as tension flees from my body thanks to the powerful jets. I place a wet cloth over my eyes and lean my head on the edge of the tub.

Several songs later, I'm singing along with Train as I pull the cloth to rewet it. My eyes flutter open against the faint light of the candles scattered around the space. I yelp at the sight male figure standing in the room.

"I'm sorry." Tyson chuckles through his sexy grin. Dimples have to be the work of the devil. At least devilish thoughts enter my mind anytime they appear on my man's face. Thoughts of licking them and nipping at them come to mind. "Ali, you okay?" Tyson kneels placing his hand in the water.

"Sorry, I am relaxed right now, my brain is slow processing," I explain.

"Can I climb in there with you?" His husky voice inquires.

"I should get out." I hold up my prune-like fingertips for his inspection. "Can you fetch me a towel?"

Tyson holds a fluffy grey towel spread wide in his arms. His dilated eyes sweep over my body as I stand from the now tepid water. His warm lips and tongue caress my neck as his arms wrap the towel around me. His lips move to my ear as I step from the tub onto the cold tile. Tyson pulls away with heavy-lidded eyes. He vigilantly dries one arm then the other. I tip his chin upward and place my seeking lips upon his. I massage his warm, plump lower lip with mine.

Too soon, he pulls away to slowly move his hands and the towel to dry my feet, calves, and then thighs. Soft moans escape as he eases closer to the apex of my thighs. He pauses his mission, looking up at me through his long dark lashes. My legs quiver. *Wow. He's my kryptonite.* Though his hands don't move, his mouth is inches away from my stomach. His warm, wet breath ignites my skin. My head falls back when his lips graze my bellybutton.

"Tyson," I moan as my fingers tangle in his hair.

"Feels good doesn't it?" He whispers, his breath is tickling my skin. His hands with the towel dry my back then my shoulders. I whimper in protest when he lifts the towel to dry my hips instead of continuing its previous route. From my hips, he wipes my stomach, my ribs, then my willpower folds.

I push his arms away, grab the sides of his head, and devour him. Though my lips are on his, I can't get close enough. I press my bare breasts to his chest—the fabric of his shirt provides the friction I desire. I lift my leg, wrapping it around his hip. Now his center meets mine.

Our tongues dance as our hands pillage, our needs seek to be met. Tyson scoops me into his arms, carries me to the bed, then lays me gently in the middle. As I lie bare on display, his eyes roam every inch of me. With great agony to me, he leisurely unbuttons his dress shirt. Beginning at his neck, one button, then two comes undone. His tongue darts out to moisten his parted lips as he slowly unfastens button three then four. His hands meet undoing one cuff then the other. I rub my thighs together trying to find the friction I desire as button five then six part. His large hands untuck his shirt all the way around.

"Tyson," my voice feels weak and raspy. "I need you."

Although he gives a low moan, he continues his slow torture. The sound of his metal belt buckle, opening sends a chill down my spine. I writhe on top his sheets, praying he hurries to join me. I stare as he unbuttons his pants and lowers his zipper. Please, please, please release your cock and join me with your pants on your thighs. But no, he removes one shoe then the other before his socks. When he lowers his slacks and steps out of each leg, I mentally urge him to hurry with his boxers. I make the gimme-gimme motions with my fingers like a toddler, my desire to touch him overwhelming.

"My fiancé is so impatient," Tyson teases before kissing his way from my shin to my thigh.

Yes, yes, just a bit higher. I feel as if I will explode at the thought of his mouth on me. "Please," I beg—shame left me long ago. My hormones are high, and I lay wanton. "Baby, I need you now," I plead.

Propped on his elbows, Tyson's lips move towards mine.

"Uh-uh," I warn. "You forgot to remove something." He chuckles before moving in for the kiss.

I murmur against his lips, "I need you naked right now." I push on his chest to no avail.

He rolls onto his back to slide his designer boxers over his powerful thighs. "Pregnancy has made you bossy," he teases.

I lick my lips at the sight of his erection. In the words of my grand-mother, I'm acting like a brazen hussy. I roll on top of him with my legs straddling his. I rise, place my hand on the base of his cock, and position him at my entrance. Maroon 5 starts blaring from my cell phone.

"No!" I screech.

Tyson's eyes are huge. "Clay will be here in ten minutes," I announce. "We need to get dressed and prepare the table."

Tyson places the head of his cock back at my opening. He stares into my eyes with his heavy-lidded. Inch by inch he fills me. It feels deep in this position. I grind myself against his pubis. *Right there. That is marvelous.*

"We need to hurry, baby," Tyson whispers.

With his hands on my hips, he helps me find a faster rhythm. Up and down, up and down. I slowly wind tighter and tighter. When he places his thumb on my nub, I explode. White, hot heat engulfs me. Fireworks burst behind my eyelids. Every muscle tightens as pulses rack my core. Tyson's hands on my hips continue our motions, which prolongs my pleasure. I feel him grind harder and deeper as he pulses inside me and erupts. I melt boneless on him and trace circles on his chest. As moments pass our breathing slows.

The ping of the elevator announces Clay's arrival. I shoot off Tyson, off the bed, and dig in my bag for an outfit. Tyson slowly exits the bed as if company didn't just enter the penthouse while we were naked. Walking to the open bedroom door, he sticks his head out, announcing to Clay we will be out in a bit. I'm mortified. Tonight, is not starting off as planned.

I take my time as I dress and put on a bit of make-up. I nervously style my hair up, then take it all down again. *Why am I nervous?* I know and socialize with all of Tyson's family. I've never had any problems. They seem to like me, too. They are excited about our engagement, and I predict they will embrace the pregnancy as well.

"Baby," Tyson slips behind me at the bathroom vanity. He wraps his arms around my waist, pulling me flush to him. "Clay is beginning to think you are avoiding him," he whispers near my ear. Goosebumps grow as a chill spreads through me. "You are gorgeous. Now come visit with Clay before everyone arrives."

I'm sure my face is redder than a tomato as I enter the kitchen area. Clay bites his lips, trying to hide his amusement. I pick up a dish towel, launching it at his face. Of course, he catches it.

"How do you feel tonight?" he asks.

Thankful my friend avoids teasing me; I lean down on the kitchen island across from him. "So far, all is well."

Tyson briefs Clay on the arrival of the chef then his family. He hands Clay money to entertain Laila and Joe with tonight, while Tyson and I talk to the family. As I hug Clay and thank him for helping out tonight, the buzzer rings signaling Tyson has a guest.

"Yes," Tyson answers.

"Chef John is here with the caterers," the doorman states.

"Thank you. Send them up," Tyson orders.

"Whoa, the caterers," Clay teases. "Aren't you special."

"I'm not special. It's called self-preservation," I inform Clay. "If I attempted to cook, we might get food poisoning. Tyson took pity on his loved ones and arranged the meal."

"You are special. Don't you ever let me hear you say differently. I'm lost without you. We both know you are the best thing that ever happened to him." Clay places a kiss on my cheek.

Tyson meets the caterers at the elevator. He points out the kitchen and dining area and tells the chef to holler if he needs anything. I walk up beside Tyson; he wraps his arm around my shoulders before introducing me to Chef John and the staff. I notice the name of a local grocery store on their chest. *Who knew my store offered such things?* I have a lot to learn to live in Tyson's world where money isn't an issue. I wonder if Chef John provides private lessons.

Apache approaches nervous of our new guests, I walk him to his bed in the living room area and order him to stay. Tyson brings a new chew bone from the pantry to entertain him. I try to stay close, so he'll be more comfortable with all the strangers in our space. Tyson whispers in my ear he was going to clean up and change clothes before his family arrives. Then he excuses himself from our guests.

"You are good for him," Clay mentions.

"It's hard to remember what life was like before he knocked me over and bathed me in kisses at the park."

"Um," Clay laughs. "I meant Tyson."

I don't know what to say to that. I feel like Tyson and Clay rescued me. The day I entered their places of business, my world felt right for the first time in a long time. From that day, positive things kept coming my way. I gained friends. I fell in love with two great kids I have the privilege of watching from time to time. Jack came to visit. I have a new car. I found full-time employment. I moved to a better apartment. I gained a boyfriend. I gained a dog. One day changed the rest of my life.

"Ali?" Clay calls to me. I guess I'm not listening. "There you are. It's the pregnancy brain fog."

"What?"

"It's in the pregnancy book."

I flinch. "You read a pregnancy book?" I'm astonished.

"My sister swore by it when she was pregnant. Quoted the damn thing all the time." Clay explains. "I asked if I could borrow it, but she'd already given her copy away. She suggested I buy it on Amazon." He shrugs. "I had to download a Kindle App to my phone because I bought the digital version. I read a bit before bed last night," he confesses and smiles at me. "I figure we spend forty hours together each week, so I need to prepare, too."

Tears fill my eyes with his kindness. When I can no longer hide my sniffles, Clay fetches me a tissue. Tyson returns asking what is wrong. I assure him it is just the pregnancy hormones. I think I hear him murmur to Clay that this may be a long nine months.

The buzzer sounds, announcing the arrival of more guests. I rise fumbling to straighten my sundress. Tyson runs a finger under a strap from my shoulder blade, up over my shoulder, pausing near my neck.

"They already love you. You look gorgeous," he whispers into my ear, his warm breath caressing me. "It's just a dinner with my family."

He's right. I know all of them, they know me—I love them all. They aren't the prim and proper, wealthy family they could be. They are normal and very down to earth. I think it's the formality of Tyson hiring a chef and staff that makes me nervous. Soon the elevator pings announcing it's show time. Tyson moves us toward the elevator with hand on my lower back.

"There they are!" Marshall Lennox announces. "My son and his new fiancé." He awards his son a one-armed man hug of congratulations. Then he hands a bottle to Tyson and a bottle to me.

"Wow! Pappy Van Winkle's Family Reserve, Marshall you shouldn't have." I lean into Tyson admiring the dark amber liquid. "My father is also a Pappy fan."

Tyson looks to me in shock. Marshall grins admiringly. "Have you sipped it?" I nod. "I knew she was a keeper." He beams at me, then Tyson.

"Priceless!" Clay doubles over in laughter at our receiving the alcohol. "This will be a fun evening." He attempts to control his laughter by deep breathing. I worry he might ruin our announcement if he can't control his laughing fit soon.

As I admire the bottle of red wine I received, I realize I won't be able to drink it for many months, Tyson's mom approaches me beaming. "Ali, darling," she greets. "We are so blessed that you will be joining our family." I'm not a huggy-person yet find myself wrapped in her embrace.

Marcia joins us with a very excited Laila. "Let's see the ring," they say in unison.

I extend my left hand, fluttering my fingers just a bit for effect. I'm thankful I joined Laila for a mani-pedi day out last week—my manicure allows me to proudly display my engagement ring.

"Grandmother's ring never looked lovelier," Marcia boasts.

"Pardon me?" In shock, I need clarification. "Is this a family heirloom?" Suddenly, I feel faint and weak-kneed.

"Tyson didn't share the story of the ring with you?" Marcia shakes her head. "Men just don't understand the importance of these things." I feel she attempts to excuse Tyson's misstep.

Tyson's mother grasps my left hand, shaking her head disapprovingly. "He is very aware of the history of this ring. In fact, when he asked permission to give it to you, we discussed it in detail."

Flabbergasted I struggle to speak. "I..." my soft voice trembles. "Let's take a seat, and you can share the story with me." I need to sit before I collapse. I want to pick up a nearby architecture magazine to fan my over-heated face, neck, and ears.

Tyson interrupts our plans. "Our dinner is nearly ready; I need to share a few items first."

Wait! What? Is he going to announce our pregnancy now? I'm not ready. I feel myself wobble. Tyson notices, quickly he stands behind me, a hand on each hip for support. In my ear, he asks if I'm okay. I nod.

"Laila and Joe," he begins as I lean back into him, his arms wrap around my waist. "Clay will be taking the two of you out for dinner and fun. So much fun, that he won't even tell me where you are going."

As the children cheer, Marcia and Stephen look for more details. Clay speaks to the two of them out of earshot. I watch as Stephen hands over his car keys, and the three bound into the elevator waving good-bye as the black doors slide closed.

"Ali and I wanted to celebrate our engagement with our adult family members tonight. Clay will have the children back when I text him our meal is wrapping up. Now, the chef assures me our meal will be divine, so let's begin. Shall we?" Tyson escorts me at his side to the formal dining room.

He pulls out a chair assisting me to sit. He then assumes the chair next to me at the head of the table. I anxiously place my napkin in my lap as the others find a seat. The caterers immediately approach delivering filled wine glasses to everyone. I quickly look to Tyson, he needs to announce it now, or drink my wine for me. He calmly clasps my hand mouthing 'grape juice' as he nods to my glass. Looking closely, I notice my beverage seems darker than the others. I only hope our guests won't see the difference.

After salad plates arrive for each of us, Tyson raises his glass. "A toast," he pauses, waiting for everyone to join with lifted glasses.

"May I?" Marshall asks. Tyson approves. "To life, laughter, and love. Ali, we are proud to welcome you to our family. Tyson, we're proud of you, son. You've found the perfect woman." He tips his glass towards us.

Crud! Tears threaten to form. *How can a pregnant woman do anything with these pesky hormones?* I sip slowly from my wine glass while trying to rein in my emotions.

Tyson pushes his chair back, clasps my hand prompting me to rise with him. "We have an announcement." He looks into my eyes before placing a chaste kiss on my lips. "We are pregnant!"

I could have heard a pin drop. The chef and his staff freeze trying not to distract from such an announcement. Tyson's mother clutches her chest, Marcia smiles at me, and Stephen high-fives Tyson.

"Well, say something," he prompts his family as I worry what this reaction means.

Simultaneously, four chairs fly back as his family comes to the head of the table to congratulate us. His mother excitedly cries, Marcia cheers promising she kept many of her children's baby clothes, while the two men pat Tyson on the back boasting of his studly-ness. I return hugs and happily smile as they celebrate our good news.

Several conversations take place at the same time. I find it difficult to follow them all. I hear Stephen claim to Tyson there was no shame in proposing with a baby on the way.

"Actually," I interrupt loudly. All eyes look to me. "There is much more to the story. As we eat, Tyson and I will share all of the details." It's important to me that they know Tyson proposed before my sharing the pregnancy news. It means more to me that Tyson proposed first. Once I figured out Jack hadn't told him, I found his proposal romantic.

As we eat, Tyson assures his family my wine glass contains sparkling grape juice before we take turns sharing the debacle that is our marriage proposal and baby announcement story. His mother claims at least we have a unique story.

I eat my entire salad but find it hard to finish half my fillet, asparagus, and roasted potatoes. I worry the rich meat, or the seasonings might haunt me later, so I don't push it. Noticing my tentative eating, Marcia inquires about morning sickness. Tyson jumps in to share I haven't felt well for over a week and experienced some morning sickness more in recent days, as his fingers lightly caress my hand at the corner of the table.

Too soon, he withdraws his hand to text Clay under the table as the staff clears the dinner plates with the promise of dessert. Staff fills coffee cups before my favorite part of the meal is revealed. Tyson shared my favorite things with the chef. He created a unique chocolate-peanut butter cheesecake for us. I moan aloud at the sight of it as the waitress slips it in front of me. Yes. Out loud in front of his entire family, soon to be my family. Embarrassment shines on my cheeks as I attempt to wait for everyone's to have theirs before I dive into mine.

"Oh my gosh," I mumble mouth full when it hits my taste buds. More inappropriate sounds escape. Tyson's eyes burn with desire watching me.

Stephen clears his throat loudly from the other side of the table.

"I am sorry," I try to express a modicum of decency.

Marcia quickly interjects that it was divine. She motions to her plate proving that she was too busy engulfing it to make appreciative sounds. She has one tiny bite left as the rest of us have only taken one bite.

Laughter fills the air. I love this family. Although I embarrassed myself, I feel comfortable in their presence. They are normal. They allow me to be me and accept me. The conversations soon return as I slowly enjoy every morsel of my dessert, as well as Tyson's.

"They will leave the leftover dessert with us," he whispers into my ear.

Suddenly I desire to straddle his lap to show my deep appreciation for his meal planning tonight. I rub my thighs together under the table. Tyson's eyes dilate knowingly. I bite my lips, shaking my head slightly. It would be rude to rush our guests out the door so that we could retire to the bedroom. I attempt to tuck away my arrant desires as we rise from the dinner table, opting for the comfort in the living room area.

Tyson and I thank the caterers and escort them to the elevator, before joining everyone in the living room. Moments after the staff left, the elevator pings again signaling Clay and the children's return.

Laila and Joe run into the space, excitedly sharing the details of their dinner and activities at the Fun Zone. Clay took his shoes off and joined them in the multi-level maze of tubes, nets, slides, and balls. They proudly display the toys they won on the games they played and share that Clay said next time Tyson and Ali plan to take them to the Fun Zone.

Clay smiles like a Cheshire cat as he places tumblers near the Pappy Van Winkle on the island. Without a word Marshall, Stephen, and Tyson join him while at the same time, Laila and Joe disappear into Uncle Tyson's game room.

"Gentleman, if I weren't carrying Tyson's baby, I'd need a glass, too," I announce.

"She is a keeper." Stephen pats his brother on the back.

Having avoided the elephant in the room long enough, Tyson's mother decided she needs answers. "Ali dear, what are your thoughts on the wedding date?"

All eyes flash to me. I'm grateful they are not laser beams, or I'd have burned to ash on the spot. Tyson senses my discomfort and returns to my side. "We've discussed it a little," I admit. Who knew once engaged we immediately needed to have all of the answers to our life plan?

Tyson wraps his arm around my shoulders. "We need a few more days before we share our options or plans." Typical man, he thinks his word will be enough to end this topic.

"Will you marry before the baby arrives or after?" His mother asks.

"You could elope, fly to Las Vegas, or plan the wedding of your dreams," Marcia adds. "Today, couples don't hide pregnancies. It's not taboo to live together or have a baby out of wedlock."

"I know." Tyson's mom defends. "I was simply trying to start a dialog to allow the two of them to make their decisions." She smiles at me. "Ali darling, I didn't mean to offend you. I simply wondered how far the two of you had discussed."

I ask Tyson to fetch me a bottle of water. "As you know, my family lives in Hannibal," I start my explanation. "I don't want to go into great detail, but it is important that you understand. My best friend and college roommate

committed suicide. I found her. So much of my life and memories in Hannibal included Leslie, so I ran. I moved to Kansas City without telling my family and friends." I take a sip of my water.

Tyson chooses to speak for me. "Her brother Jack knows she is here. In fact, he came to visit recently. Ali needed to start over someplace where every building, business, and house didn't remind her of her friend." He swipes the back of his fingers over my cheek.

"It's only been a year," Clay chimes in, "I for one, am proud of how well Ali has recovered from her tragedy." He offers me a fist-bump on his way for a refill.

"So, you see I need to decide if I am ready to contact my parents. My brother claims they have discussed my disappearance often and seemed to understand the importance of my leaving." I shrug and pinch my lips. "As Leslie and I were inseparable, my parents and her parents were close. Our families are neighbors, and we vacationed together, spent holidays together—you name it we all did it together."

"We need some more time," Tyson states ending this conversation with authority.

"Well, know that we are here for anything you might need and anxiously await to plan the wedding with you," Marcia informs with a slight smile.

The conversation seamlessly flows to other topics. I kiss Tyson then excuse myself to check on the kids. I join Laila and Joe at the air-hockey table. Joe informs me of the rules and techniques as they continue their match. I laugh with them and cheer when each score.

"So, when do we go buy my dress for your wedding?" Laila asks while keeping her eyes trained on the puck.

"Uncle Tyson and I are still making plans. As soon as we know the date, we will plan a girls' shopping day."

Laila cheers at the happy news.

"Can we call you Aunt Ali, now?" Joe asks.

I don't mind, but I'm not sure what the protocol on this might be. I want to defer to his parents, but they aren't in here.

"Mom says we needed to ask your permission." Laila supplies.

"I would be honored to be Aunt Ali," I announce hugging each one of them.

"Uh-hmm," Tyson interrupts from the door. "What's going on in here?"

"I'm telling Aunt Ali how to play air-hockey," Joe announces proudly.

"Aunt Ali, huh?" Tyson teases pulling me tight to his side.

"She's marrying you so she will be our aunt. Mom says it's okay to practice calling her Aunt Ali," Laila informs. "I've always wanted an aunt." She wraps her arms around my waist. "Mommy and I thought Uncle Tyson would never get married and I would live my entire life without an aunt."

I attempt to trap my laughter inside by placing my fingers over my mouth. Tyson acts offended. I lose my battle with the giggles when a loud snort slips out my nostrils. Yes. I snorted. Nice. Tyson and the kids giggle uncontrollably at my snort. Joe runs from the game room to inform all adults that Aunt Ali snorted. Laila follows him out still giggling.

"I love you, future Mrs. Lennox." Tyson wraps one arm around my waist and one across my chest while pulling my back tight against his chest. "I love how easy you are around my family and the kids. I love the sounds you make when you eat chocolate-peanut butter cheese-cake, and I love that my baby is growing inside you right now."

"I love you, too," I whisper.

"Tyson! Ali! We are leaving!" Laila yells from the living room.

"Let's get rid of my family, so I can show you just how much I love you," Tyson whispers into my ear before taking my hand to lead me to the family.

We share many good-byes, share hugs, and promise to contact them soon with any details. We wave good-bye to a full elevator as the doors slide shut.

Tyson swoops my legs out from under me and whisks me to the bedroom.

EPILOGUE

Ali:

I peek through the heavy blinds at the backyard. Guests fill nearly all of the white folding chairs on the lawn. Our small, private ceremony will begin in mere minutes. Shortly, I will become Tyson's wife. I jump at the calling of my name, the blinds slam shut with a wooden clonk.

"You shouldn't be peeking," Marcia admonishes me. She straightens a pleat on the front of her royal blue dress. "Any minute Marshall will knock on our door signaling the men have taken their places. You know you aren't supposed to see Tyson until you are on the patio."

I smile at my soon-to-be sister-in-law. "How do I look?" I ask.

"Like a princess!" Laila cheers from my side. "Mom looks like a queen, me and you look like princesses." She continues to spin enjoying the flare of her blue dress.

"You are the prettiest princess I've ever seen," I inform her as the knock we are anticipating arrives.

"It's time! It's time!" Laila screams. "I get to be a flower girl in my princess dress. Hurry, we need to go."

Internally, I'm as excited as Laila. I expected to be nervous. I'm not nervous—I'm excited to start my new role as Tyson's wife and soon a mother.

Laila walks with her grandfather from the master bedroom down the stairs. Marcia leads me, and I follow. I carry my bouquet in one hand and my heels in the other. I refuse to attempt these stairs in my dress and heels. I'm just an accident waiting to happen.

Right on cue, Laila emerges from the sheers, holding Joe's hand. Clay locks arms with Marcia escorting her close behind the ringbearer and flower girl. At the first notes of The Wedding March, Marshall and I began our journey towards his son, my future husband, and father of my baby.

I planned to smile at each of the two rows on my left and right as we stepped closer and closer to Tyson. Once my eyes find my man in his tux waiting for me, I can't tear my eyes away. I feel like I must drag Marshall to hurry up. I can't get to Tyson fast enough.

Marshall kisses my cheek and whispers 'welcome to our family' in my ear before he extends my hand with his to Tyson. Tyson's hand shoots sparks of fire up my arm straight to my heart. Tears pool in my eyes at the love I find in his. He mouths 'I love you' as he squeezes my hand.

I don't hear the words spoken by the minister, the exchanging of the vows and rings, or any of the ceremony. Thoughts of my life with Tyson crowd my mind. I dream of the months to come, my belly swelling, and our planning for the arrival of our little one. We walk Apache and play in the park. We decorate a nursery and attend birthing classes. So many exciting things are coming in our near future.

"Ladies and Gentlemen, I give you Mr. and Mrs. Tyson Lennox. You may now kiss the bride."

My thoughts vanish. Tyson places his hands on my hips pulling me into him. I can hear cheers from his family and friends as his lips feed on mine. I part my lips allowing him access to every part of me. He accepts the invitation; his tongue plunders as my hands clutch tighter to his hair.

"Uncle Ty-thon, that's enough!" Joe hollers.

Tyson pulls away. I giggle at Joe's scrunched up face with tongue sticking out. Someday, he won't think kisses so repulsive. Marcia returns my bouquet, and we trot down our short aisle. Tyson pulls me through the sheers into the house. He doesn't stop there. He quickly opens the front door, pulls me through, and closes it again.

"What are we doing?" I laugh.

"I need a moment alone with you," he admits.

I can't argue with my new husband. I need more, too. The kiss ignites a fire, and I desire more, much more. We're all hands and mouths, groping and kissing, sucking and nibbling. He needs me, and I need him. Unable to keep my balance I lean back against the front door. I fist his hair, his hand at the small of my back pulls my pelvis tight to his. I moan. He growls.

His father opens the front door; I nearly fall inside. Tyson ends our make-out session in time to hold me up. "I found them," Marshall yells into the house then shakes his head. "Your mother is tearing the house apart looking for you, and the kids think you are playing hide-and-seek."

I attempt to put myself back together. Tyson whispers. "Not a hair out of place. You are gorgeous, Mrs. Lennox." He places a peck on my earlobe.

As we make our way back to the patio, my cheeks heat. I'm sure Stephen will tease me about this for years to come.

On the patio, we take the seats of honor at the head table between Clay and Marcia. The umbrellas add color and help protect us from the hot summer sun. Laila and Joe join us asking where we were hiding. Tyson claims we were on the patio the entire time waiting on them.

As the brain fog from Tyson's kisses fades, I look at the three tables filled with our family and closest friends. I gasp, clutching my hands to my chest. *It can't be. Uh-uh.* I fan my face trying to shake the delusion.

"Breathe," Tyson's low murmur encourages. "Breathe in and out. Easy." He turns my face to his. "Look at me." He waits for my eyes to focus on him. "Okay?"

I nod. Tyson calms me instantly. He allows me to regain my composure.

"I should have told you. I know you hate surprises, but..." He clears his throat. "I'm sorry, we had to surprise you. Otherwise, you would have refused."

"Tyson, my parents are here." It's a statement and a question at the same time. I still believe my mind is playing tricks on me. "Leslie's parents..."

"Please don't be mad at me. I had to invite them. They needed to be here. I had to do this for you." He searches for my reaction, my anger, but only finds my fear.

"They plan to stay at their table. If you are ready, I mean when you are ready, I will walk over there with you." His hands caress my arms and back to soothe me.

Clay kneels beside us. "You are the strongest person I know. You've experienced so much. You did what you needed to survive. You gave up everything and started a new life. That shows your inner strength. You have healed this past year. I know it, Tyson knows it, Jack knows it. It's time that you realize it." He pats my hand. "I've spoken to them. They are just as scared as you are. They love you and miss you. You can do this. As your best man, I order you to drink some water, pull on your big girl panties, and introduce your husband to your family."

"What if I'm not wearing any panties?" I whisper.

Tyson chokes on his water. Clay pats his back as he coughs and gasps for air.

"You might not want to mention that fact to your parents," Clay warns. "You've got this."

I look at Tyson. "You think I should?" He nods. "You'll stay by my side the entire time?" He nods. "I'm scared," I confess. I rise from my chair and straighten my dress to stall a bit longer. Tyson takes my hand and clasps his fingers into mine. "I love you." I place my free hand on the back of his neck pulling him toward my lips. I need him. I need all of him. As we keep our kiss rated-PG, I feel my strength return. I pull away not letting go of his neck. "Let's go."

With Tyson by my side, I can do anything. In the following months, my family and I reunite. Tyson and I spent a long weekend in Hannibal. It was an exhausting visit for me emotionally. With memories of Leslie and my pregnancy hormones, I was an emotional mess.

The four parents visited KC each month. They took me shopping for maternity clothes and baby gear. They helped with the nursery at home, and the mini-nursery Clay insisted on creating in the office at the gym. Jack chose to play baseball at a KC metro community college. This gave us games to attend and my parents another reason to visit us.

In March, six days past my due date, my water broke as I walked Apache in the park. I called Clay, and he activated the phone tree. Why did I call Clay and not my husband? Tyson now teaches history, economics, and government at Staley High School. Although he had a plan in place at the school, it's quicker for Clay to call Tyson and he meet us at the hospital.

With military precision my go bag joined me at the hospital, Tyson and Clay's family arrived, escorted Apache home, Tyson joined me in the labor room, then Jack and my parents came before Baby Boy Lennox's arrived.

My life is everything I would have ever hoped for. I've learned a lot in the past two years. I am still the strong young women I was prior to Leslie's suicide. I've learned to embrace the good memories and learn from the bad. I've learned to balance my friendships and relationships with some time of my own.

My decision between boxers and briefs was an easy one. I chose both. I work with my boxer and married my brief-reading lawyer.

The End

WANT MORE? FOLLOW ME:

Keep up on the latest news and new releases from Haley Rhoades.
Text: Frogs to 33777

Please consider leaving a quick review on Amazon and Goodreads.

BOXERS OR BRIEFS TRIVIA

All names used in this book
are famous boxers and lawyers.

Boxers
Mohammad Ali, Laila Ali, Cassius Clay, George Foreman, Mike Tyson,
Floyd Mayweather, Joe Louis, Joe Frazier, Ray Leonard, Lennox Lewis,
Ray Jones, Jack Dempsey, Bernard Hopkins

Lawyers
Marcia Clark, Johnnie Cochran, Gloria Allred, Thurgood Marshall,
Leslie Abramson, Stephen Breyer, Clarence Thomas

ABOUT THE AUTHOR

About Haley Rhoades

Haley Rhoades's writing is another bucket-list item coming to fruition, just like meeting Stephen Tyler and skydiving. As she continues to write romance and young adult books, she plans to complete her remaining bucket-list items, including ghost-hunting, storm-chasing, and bungee jumping. She is a Netflix-binging, Converse-wearing, avidly-reading, traveling geek.

A team player, Haley thrived as her spouse's career moved the family of four eight times to three states. One move occurred eleven days after a C-section. Now with two adult sons, Haley copes with her newly emptied nest by writing and spoiling Nala, her Pomsky. A fly on the wall might laugh as she talks aloud to her fur-baby all day long.

Haley's under five-foot, fun-size stature houses a full-size attitude. Her uber-competitiveness in all things entertains, frustrates, and challenges family and friends. Not one to shy away from a dare, she faces the consequences of a lost bet no matter the humiliation. Her fierce loyalty extends from family, to friends, to sports teams.

Haley's guilty pleasures are Lifetime and Hallmark movies. Her other loves include all things peanut butter, *Star Wars*, mathematics, and travel. Past day jobs vary tremendously from an elementary special-education para-professional, to a YMCA sports director, to a retail store accounting department, and finally a high school mathematics teacher.

Haley resides with her husband and fur-baby in the Kansas City area. This Missouri-born girl enjoys the diversity the Midwest offers.

Reach out on Facebook, Twitter, Instagram, or her website...she would love to connect with her readers.

amazon.com/author/haleyrhoades

goodreads.com/HaleyRhoadesAuthor

bookbub.com/authors/haley-rhoades

facebook.com/authorhaleyrhoades

twitter.com/HaleyRhoadesBks

instagram.com/HaleyRhoadesAuthor

pinterest.com/haleyrhoadesaut

Made in the USA
Monee, IL
03 July 2021